STREET AFFILIATED PUBLISHING LLC
A Hustla'z Life
REVENGE
2
A NOVEL BY:
LAZ

A Hustla'z Life 2:
Revenge

Published by: Street Affiliated Publishing, L.L.C. all associated logos are property of Street Affiliated Publishing, L.L.C.

Editor: Progressive Editing Solutions, L.L.C.
Join us on our social network pages:
Facebook
Author LAZ
Printed in the United States

DEDICATED TO ALL OF MY READERS. YOU ARE MY WORLD. I HOPE YOU TRULY ENJOY THIS BOOK.

Presents

A Hustla'z Life 2: Revenge

LAZ

STREET AFFILIATED

STREET AFFILIATED PUBLISHING LLC
A Hustla'z
LIFE
REVENGE
2
A NOVEL BY:
LAZ

ONE

"Hannibal Watson having completed the ninety days' probation that I previously ordered you to serve under the supervision of the Oklahoma Department of Corrections without any violations, I do hereby release you from their supervision. I reluctantly order that you be allowed to serve out the remainder of your probation without supervision," Judge Carlos Harris stated as he looked at Hannibal over the top of his glasses. "Although there's no proof, I personally do not believe that you have adhered to the terms of your probation." Judge Harris said in finality before banging his gavel. "You are free to go."

Adjourning the court, Judge Carlos Harris returned to his chambers.

A slight smile curved Hannibal's mouth, knowing Judge Harris had been one-hundred percent correct in his statement. If they only knew the magnitude of his plans, they would tack on another ten years to his sentence to keep him off the streets.

Two weeks and four murders later, every hustla and gangsta in the City of Tulsa and the surrounding area were wondering if they are going to be next on the kill list. The city had never seen a series of murders that were so brutal. The last murder was committed in the parking garage of the *Promenade Mall.* J-Rock, who was big in everything from drugs to prostitution, was left with his throat slit from ear-to-ear on the trunk of his Cadillac CTS.

The powers that be knew these murders were no coincidence, but no one could put the pieces together to come up with who was giving the orders and why. Every time a body turned up a couple more would surface due to baseless retaliation attempts. This type of pointless violence made sense to the hustla'z and gangsta's, but the working public and politicians were even more confused as to what was going on and how to view the situation. Some viewed the murderer and the murders as a good public service. After all, those that were being murdered were young, black, and thugs. They looked at those being killed as one less criminal to pollute the streets. With that frame of mind so prevalent throughout the area, no politician or law enforcement officer would take an overly tough stance against what was happening. Of course, they went through the motions for the media because they had to show face, but they did nothing more.

Throughout all this confusion, Hannibal's organization only grew stronger. With very little resistance, he was quietly able to make moves on all the dead hustla'z businesses. He incorporated the disenfranchised members of those crews into *Hustla'z Inc.* while keeping the organization itself a secret from everyone except a chosen few consisting of Lamar, Bey, Gunslanger, Murder, Wild Bill, Lord Jamar, and OJ. Everyone below them had no idea who they were really working for. Hannibal did this to insulate himself and the head members from prosecution and retaliation while still providing a great amount of organization to things.

Hannibal himself dropped off the scene totally. He was never seen making any deals. No longer were they nickel and diming in the streets like typical hustla'z. They now served as the men that supplied the mid to low level hustla'z. However, the longstanding saying held true that with more money comes more problems.

The deadline for the kill list to be completed was approaching, and there was only one other person left to be taken care of. Hannibal could not be more pleased with the work that his hired killer Wind had put in. The man was a true assassin in every sense of the word and was worth every penny that he was paid. Hannibal knew that he had to meet up with Wind in order to make the final payment. Hannibal hoped to be able to call on Wind in the future if someone got in the way of what he was trying to do. During that meeting, he also had a small piece of business to discuss with Dee.

Ring! Ring! Ring!

The ringing of Hannibal's phone broke his joyful moment, knowing that another enemy had been eliminated. Without hesitation, he grabbed his cell phone off his coffee table, thinking it was Lamar calling to check on him. Since he had successfully completed his probation and was able to tell the judge to go fuck off he had been spending less time in Tulsa.

He answered the phone, and said, "Speak!"

"Hey baby, how are you doing?" a cheerful female asked with excitement.

"I'm good, but who is this?" Hannibal asked, being that he failed to recognize the voice of the female on the other end.

"Oh, so did you already forgotten about your new Bonnie?" the young lady inquired.

Finally recognizing who he was talking to, Hannibal giggled, and said, "Nah, I haven't forgot about you. What's up wit'cha?"

"Nothing, just trying to get wit' you. I haven't seen you in a minute. Where the hell you been?" Andrea asked, knowing that Hannibal had to have been up to his usual hustle game.

"I been around. Just been trying to stay out the way. Shit is a little hectic out here right now," he told her.

"I know all about it, but I'm not worried about that shit. I was calling because I need my medicine. Plus, I think you owe me some quality time anyway," Andrea reminded him.

"I don't owe you shit, but I don't have a problem kickin' it wit' you for a bit. What you up to now?"

"I'm at home fixing my daughter something to eat," Andrea stated as she stared at her daughter. "Her father will be here to pick her up soon so you can come by after that."

"I'm in OKC so it will take a minute for me to get to you, but that shit you said still doesn't tell me a time," Hannibal stated.

"Well, I'm really not feeling your attitude right now so why don't you come by here at about eleven. That will give you a chance to get your mind right and that will be the perfect time for a booty call," Andrea stated, cutting through all the bullshit.

"Ain't shit wrong wit' my mind, but that's cool wit' me. Text me the address," Hannibal said before he hung up, ending the call.

Hannibal knew Andrea was full of shit so he didn't sweat her smart-ass remarks. He only smiled at the thought of hitting that fat ass.

Before he got ready to head out for his late-night rendezvous with Andrea he decided to call Lamar to let him know he would be stopping through to speak with him. He dialed his cousin's phone number and waited for him to answer as he flipped through the channels on his TV.

"Yo, what's up, cuz?" Lamar asked when he answered the phone.

"I was calling to let you know I'll be in Tulsa in a bit. I need you to stop by Michelle's apartment so we can talk. The bullshit is almost over and we need to get ready to spread out and really get at this money."

"I'm ready and the boys are ready too. All this bullshit got everybody shook," Lamar stated.

"Well, we about to be able to put that shit to bed. Meet me over there at about nine o'clock and we'll work out the details."

"I'll be there. Later," Lamar said before he hung up the phone.

*****

Hannibal made it to his sister's apartment at about six o'clock. He took a hot shower and then dozed off to sleep on the couch with the hopes of getting some rest before his busy evening. He was awakened by the sound of his cell phone ringing off the hook. He tried to ignore it but whoever it was kept calling back-to-back. He finally grabbed the phone and saw it was Keisha calling and decided to go ahead and take the call.

"What's so goddamn important that you keep blowing up my phone?" Hannibal asked, slightly irritated.

"Hannibal, I need to see you. It's important. There's some shit going down and I can't tell you over the phone," Keisha told him, trying to stress the importance of what she had to say.

"Well, it's going to have to wait until later 'cause I'm 'bout to handle a little business," Hannibal stated, down playing her request because he figured she was only trying to get him to come over to her crib to spend some time with her.

"Yo, this ain't no bullshit! You need to hear this! Stop fucking around, Hannibal!" Keisha yelled.

"First off you need to remember who the fuck you talkin' to, and stop yelling at me through this phone," Hannibal said, pausing to let his words sink in before he continued. "Now, unless you dying your shit is going to have to wait. I have plans and I can't be in two places at once. I'll be at your place by nine so have your ass there. Peace!" Hannibal stated, and then he ended the call before she could reply.

Hannibal reached over and decided to help himself to the half smoked blunt that was in the ashtray on his sister's coffee table. He lit the blunt up and took a long pull off of it. He held the smoke in for about five seconds then he exhaled. Just as he did so he could hear a knock at the door. He knew it had to be Lamar so he got up to unlock the door.

"What up, dough?" Lamar shouted as he came through the door, imitating the guys from the movie *8 Mile*.

Hannibal gave him some dap, and then said, "Come on with the jokes. We got a lot of shit to talk about, and I want to do it while Michelle isn't here."

"Alright cuz, let's get to it then. What's on your mind?" Lamar asked as he took a seat on the couch.

Hannibal took a seat on the recliner across from Lamar, and started by saying, "As you know I'm the one who is responsible for the killings that have been taking place, and that mess is about to come to an end. I didn't tell you more about that on purpose, and I'm still not going to tell you."

"We all knew who was responsible. The fucked-up part was not knowing who was next, but now it all makes sense."

Hannibal didn't tell him everything because life had taught him not to totally trust anyone and Wind being his secret hitman was his ace to pull any time he needed him even if it came to using him against Lamar.

"What I do want to talk about is how Hustla'z Inc. is going to be organized from now on. Me, you, Bey, Gunslanger, Wild Bill, Murder, Lord Jamar, and OJ will all have specific responsibilities, and we are the only ones that should know the name Hustla'z Inc. You will be second in charge and oversee distribution of all the drugs and everybody involved. Bey will be in charge of the collection of all the money and he will oversee the trap houses. Wild Bill and Gunslanger will be in charge of muscle for the entire operation. Keep an eye on Gunslanger and make sure he stays on point. I don't want his crazy ass causing trouble," Hannibal said as he started to light the blunt again.

"Man, I wouldn't worry about Gunslanger. He's crazy but he ain't stupid. He knows better than to fuck up. I will put a bullet in his head and kiss his mother at his funeral," Lamar stated with a grin.

Hannibal shook his head, and said, "No that is what you won't do. From now on our hands don't get dirty because of that type of shit unless we have to. If somebody needs to be dealt with bring it to me and I will have the situation solved. You have to understand that murders are the only time when shit gets real ugly for us. The less were directly involved in it the better off we are."

"Damn, you have this shit all thought out. When did you have time to do all that?" Lamar asked with a slight giggle.

"In two years, you have a lot of time to think. Now, Lord Jamar and OJ will oversee everything else. They can move us into the club and entertainment business since they know those type of people already. Dee is going to be available when we need deadly muscle but only on a as needed basis. I want him close but not too close so keep him out of our business. I will be taking our profits and be moving us into some legitimate businesses and expanding our organization into the south. Do you remember Darlene?" Hannibal asked.

"Yeah, I remember her. You're talking about the DA's daughter, right?" Lamar asked to confirm he was talking about the right girl.

"Yeah, that's her. She has always liked me and with her legitimate contacts she can put our money to use in places we can't. Plus, if she gets down with us she may be able to keep the law away from us too," Hannibal told him with a sly grin.

"And how do you think she can do that?"

"If she's dirty from fucking with us, we can use her to put her father in our back pocket. If some fucked up shit comes down about daddy's little girl it's bound to blow back on him. The nigga wants to be mayor so he will probably do anything to keep his name clean. A little shit to blackmail him with doesn't hurt," Hannibal concluded.

"Man, that shit sounds good to me. Tell her fine ass to hook me up with one of her downtown friends. I'll send the bitch back walking funny," Lamar said, laughing.

"I hear you. I need to get out of here. Keisha called takin' 'bout she needs to talk to me so I gotta drive all the way out there to see what the fuck she wants. Then I have that chick Andrea lined up for later," Hannibal said with a slight smile.

"So, she finally called?"

"Yeah, she called and had the nerves to try and talk slick. I shut that shit down real quick. You know how I get down," Hannibal stated as he got up and grabbed his keys.

"I'm about to head over to Sharel's house now."

"Tell her I said what's up. I'll holla at you later. Make sure everyone keeps laying low until I give the word," Hannibal said as he turned and locked the door behind them.

"Alright bro. I got it covered."

*****

Hannibal hopped on to the highway and made his way to Keisha's house in Okmulgee. Her neighborhood was extremely quiet. Hannibal slowly walked up to Keisha's door and knocked on it just loud enough for her to hear him. He only had an hour and a half before he was supposed to be at Andrea's house so he hoped she would make this quick.

Keisha answered the door and she was obviously disturbed by something. She did not look her usual beautiful self and she did not greet Hannibal with any type of affection as she always did.

"Keisha, what's so important that you had to talk to me in person?" Hannibal asked, noticing a look of concern that became more-and-more evident on her face.

"Hannibal, this dude keeps coming by the house threatening me," she said, raising her voice slightly to let Hannibal know that she was serious. "His name is Twin, and he keeps coming by here talking 'bout if I don't tell him who killed his cousins he's going to kill me. He gave me one more week to come up with the information. You know I'm not going to tell him shit, but this mutha'fucka is scaring the shit out of me."

"How in the hell does this nigga even think that you know something about his peeps? Have you been running your fuckin' mouth? I specifically told you to keep your mouth shut," Hannibal said curiously, sensing that some unwanted drama could be about to get out of hand.

"'Cause that night that it happened Monk's girlfriend told him I knew who did it," Keisha replied, staring at Hannibal with teary eyes.

"A'ight, well where does this nigga live or hang at?" Hannibal asked, convinced that he needed to eliminate Twin before Keisha folded under pressure and brought trouble to him and the organization.

Hannibal also saw this as a chance to give Dee his start at putting in work for the organization.

"I hear he hangs out somewhere around forty-sixth street north in Tulsa, but I don't know exactly where," Keisha replied, feeling a small sense of relief, knowing that Hannibal was going to deal with the situation.

"A'ight, babygirl, say no more. Don't worry about nothin'. You just take care of yourself, and I'll be in touch later. Oh, and by the way, keep it tight for me," Hannibal said with a lustful grin, and then he tapped her on the ass before he turned to walk back out the door.

Hannibal pulled off from Keisha's house and immediately grabbed his cell phone to call Andrea to let her know that he was still coming even though he was going to be a little late.

"Hello," Andrea softly answered after the second ring.

"What's up wit'cha?"

"I know your calling to tell me you can't make it so get it over with," Andrea replied with an attitude even though she was in her I'm ready to fuck mood.

"Nah, slow down babygirl. I was calling to tell you that I'm on my way. I had some unexpected business to go handle. I'm about forty-five minutes away from you so I'll see you in just a little bit," Hannibal said with a smile.

"Alright, that sounds good to me. It's your world," Andrea stated, trying to stroke Hannibal's ego as much as possible so that he would fall for her completely.

About forty minutes later, Hannibal pulled up in front of Andrea's house. As he did so he spotted six dudes chilling across the street, talking and watching every move he made.

Hannibal mumbled to himself, "I hope these niggas don't try no bullshit 'cause I got my Desert Eagle for that ass."

Hannibal beeped the horn to let her know he was outside so that she would come to the door so that he would not have to wait for her to answer it. He thought it was always best to be cautious when you are outnumbered so heavily.

He moved to step out of his car as he noticed Andrea opening her front door and waving for him to come in. He placed his Desert Eagle in his jacket pocket and hopped out of his new Mercedes-Benz SLR. As he walked towards the door he was surprised to see a 6'3", two hundred and fifteen pound, dark-skinned dude, wearing a black hoodie, blue jeans, and a pair of Timberland boots standing behind Andrea.

The guy pushed his way in front of Andrea, and asked, "What's up, playa?"

"Yo, I'm here to see Andrea," Hannibal replied calmly, thinking something wasn't right about the dude standing in front of him.

Hannibal's defenses went up just in case something foul was about to go down.

"Who are you?" the big dude asked with an attitude, immediately sizing Hannibal up.

The dude thought to himself, *Who the fuck does this lame ass nigga think he is, coming around here asking to see my girl?*

"I'm Hannibal. Why?" Hannibal started to question the dude but was stopped when Andrea stepped in front of him.

"Come in Hannibal, and Kevin don't be questioning my company," Andrea blasted off.

Hannibal walked by both of them into the house and stood in the living room.

"Fuck all that! I just don't like you havin' all these punks around my daughter," Kevin shot back at Andrea while mean mugging Hannibal.

"Anyway, nigga! What do you mean all these punks? I don't ever have anybody coming over here, and if I did it ain't none of yo' damn business!" Andrea shouted at Kevin defensively while rolling her eyes and throwing her hands on her hips.

While they were going back and forth Hannibal was becoming more-and-more irritated with the way that Kevin was looking at him with every second that passed.

"Alright Andrea, don't be trying to front 'cause you know I will smack the shit out of you," Kevin warned her, trying not to look soft in front of Hannibal. "Brittany, come out that room so we can go!" Kevin shouted as he turned his attention back to Hannibal. "Sucker ass nigga," he whispered under his breath as he turned to walk out the door.

"Say bruh, you got somethin' you want to say to me?" Hannibal asked, challenging Kevin to say what was really on his mind.

Hannibal was more than prepared to go toe-to-toe with this nigga, especially since he was bragging about hitting on a woman and being disrespectful.

"What you mean, homie? If I had somethin' to say I would say it," Kevin stated as he turned around to face Hannibal.

"Bruh, I don't know you and it's obvious that you don't know me. I'm not trying to get in y'all business, but when you start directing your shit towards me then that's somethin' else. You feel me?" Hannibal asked Kevin to make sure he understood what he was trying to say as they looked at each other directly in the eyes.

Andrea could sense that things were about to get out of hand so she jumped in between them, and said, "Kevin, get the fuck out of here before you end up starting some shit."

"Fuck that nigga!" Kevin stated as he picked his daughter up off the ground and carried her to his truck that was parked in the driveway.

After he got Brittany into her car seat, Kevin walked across the street to where the other guys were standing. As he talked to the guys, he kept glancing back towards Andrea's house and Hannibal could see everything through the living room window.

"Yo, Andrea, I don't know what's up with that fool, but he obviously don't know who the fuck he's talkin' to 'cause it's hammer time with me," Hannibal popped off in anger. "What the fuck was he doing here anyway? I thought you said he would be gone by now."

"I did say that but he was late, and she really wanted to go. I didn't know he was going to be talkin' shit."

Hannibal had to remind himself that he said he was putting unnecessary drama behind him, but he also knew that if something did go down there was a high chance that he would have to use his gun to get out of it. He decided to give Lamar a call to give him his location just in case he needed him.

Hannibal pulled his cell phone from his pocket and speed dialed Lamar's phone number.

Three rings later, Lamar answered his cell phone, and asked, "What's up, cuz?"

"Yo, I'm over the girl Andrea's crib in the Hills and her baby daddy and some other fools might be trying to start some beef. I don't want to shoot nobody so I might need y'all to pass through. You feel me?"

"I'm on it, cuz. Just hit me if you need me and I'm there," Lamar confirmed, sensing the seriousness in his cousin's voice.

"A'ight, peace," Hannibal said before he ended the call.

Just as he was about to return his attention to Andrea there was a series of hard knocks at the door. Hannibal just shook his head because he couldn't believe the amount of traffic that was passing through Andrea's house at this time of night. *What the fuck is going on?* he thought to himself.

TWO

Knock! Knock! Knock!

Dee leaned in closer to Andrea's door, hoping to get the heads-up on who was inside.

Andrea opened the door, and said, "Hey, bro! Come in."

"What's up, sis?" Dee asked as he stepped into Andrea's house and noticed the excitement on her face.

"Nothin' much. Just dealing with the usual bullshit," Andrea replied as she closed the door. "Hey bro, I want you to meet someone."

Andrea and Dee both turned to face Hannibal who was standing there waiting for Dee to recognize him.

"Shit, no introduction needed. I already know him. What's up, playboy?" Dee inquired with a curious smile, being shocked to see Hannibal kicking it with his sister.

"I'm not up to nothin'. Just visiting the pretty young lady here," Hannibal said with a smile.

"I see you got little sis on your team, huh?" Dee asked with a giggle as he winked at Andrea.

"Oh, I see y'all know each other," Andrea interjected with a smile.

"Yeah, I know him. I'm actually glad to see you. Andrea give us a minute 'cause we have some unfinished business to deal with," Hannibal said as he looked at Dee to back him up.

Dee nodded his head towards Andrea to let her know that it was cool.

"Ok, but keep in mind that me and you still have some business to deal with too," Andrea jokingly remarked with laughter, and then she walked towards her bedroom, leaving Hannibal and Dee staring at each other with seriousness on their faces.

"Now, what's up, Hannibal?" Dee asked, sensing that Hannibal had something serious on his mind.

"First of all, I appreciate the help you gave me. Now check this out," Hannibal started as his facial expression changed, "you know Andrea's baby daddy, right?"

"Yeah, I know the nigga. Not to sit down and talk to but you know how it is," Dee told him.

"Well, homeboy must be pussy whipped or he has a death wish 'cause I just came over here to visit shorty and dude started shitting out his mouth bad. He was shootin' off at the mouth and then he bounced outside to put his little crew on point. I'm not trying to make your niece an orphan, but you know that bullshit is a no-no," Hannibal explained.

"Bro, don't sweat that nigga. He is all bark and no bite. He was just frontin' 'cause he can't stand to see her with somebody else. Plus, don't shit go down around here without me being on it. You feel me?" Dee stressed as he cracked a smile. "As a matter of fact, let's take a walk outside real quick. Yo, sis, we'll be right back!"

They headed out the door and over to where Kevin and his crew were standing and talking. They were passing around several blunts and having a few laughs. Dee and Hannibal approached them, and then the laughter stopped and frowns covered all of their faces.

"What's up, fellas?" Dee asked as he cracked a slight grin.

"Same ole shit different day," one of the guys who respected Dee replied with a smile.

"Look here, Kevin, we need to talk real quick so why don't we take a walk across the street," Dee suggested as he motioned with his hands in that direction.

"Cool," Kevin agreed as he nodded his head. "Yo, Greg, don't smoke all my shit 'cause I'll be right back!"

They walked across the street to where Dee's car was parked then he turned, and said, "Yo, Kevin, this is my man Hannibal and if you got a problem with him you bring it to me 'cause you runnin' off at the mouth on some of your bullshit won't end well. You feel me?"

"Yeah, I feel you, Dee," Kevin replied in a low tone of voice as he nodded his head in agreement. "My bad, Hannibal. I shouldn't have let Andrea get in my head."

Fuck this nigga, Kevin thought to himself as he faked an apology in order to keep the peace between himself and Dee.

"I feel you, bruh. I know how that baby mama bullshit goes," Hannibal responded as he hit knuckles with Kevin.

"Now, Kevin, why don't you go and get my niece out this night air before she catches a cold," Dee suggested but it sounded more like an order.

"You know I'm gonna take care of her," Kevin stated as he turned and walked towards his truck.

Kevin, without giving a second thought to his crew across the street, got into his truck, backed out of the driveway, and drove down the street as Hannibal and Dee watched.

Dee turned his attention back to Hannibal, and said, "Man, I'm 'bout to roll out. I need to lay it down."

"Before you go, I have another piece of business I need to talk to you about. I wanted to know if you'd be interested in handling some contract work for me from time-to-time. Nothin' heavy, just a lightweight every once and a while," Hannibal told him.

"I don't have a problem with that. Just get at me and I'm on it."

"I should have somethin' for you real soon so I'll be in touch," Hannibal told him as they hit knuckles, and then he walked back towards the house.

Hannibal walked back into Andrea's house to find her sleep on her couch. It was past midnight now and he was tired himself so he decided to lock the door behind himself, chalk the night up as a loss, and head over to his sister's apartment for the evening.

*****

The next day Hannibal woke up at his sister's apartment and decided that he would give a day with Andrea another try. He picked up the phone to give her a call and see what she was up to.

Three rings later Andrea picked up the phone, and said, "Hello!"

"This is Hannibal. I wanted to see what you had planned for the day. I thought maybe we could take a little ride and spend the day together."

"That sounds cool with me since last night got messed all the way up," Andrea replied.

"Well, get ready and I will be there as fast as I can," Hannibal stated before he ended the call.

Thirty minutes later, while Andrea was peeping through her window awaiting Hannibal's arrival, he pulled into Andrea's view. She hastily walked outside and got into the passenger's seat.

"Well, you ready to ride out?" Hannibal asked with a smile.

"Yes, baby! I'm really in need of some quality time," Andrea replied, returning Hannibal's smile.

Andrea thought to herself, *Yeah, we'll spend some quality time since you'll be a dead nigga real soon.*

"True," Hannibal stated as he turned to head towards the highway. He was heading towards Houston, Texas where he had just bought a house.

Cruising the highway four hours later, while Hannibal was listening to his CD player that was blasting Maxwell's CD he looked over to notice that Andrea was deep in thought.

Hannibal turned down his CD player, and asked, "Hey, babygirl, what's on your mind?"

"Nothing much. I just need a drink," Andrea replied calmly.

Andrea smiled towards Hannibal as she thought to herself, *It is a shame that a good looking brotha is going to have to fall victim to the game.*

"No problem. I got some Crown Royal in the trunk, but if you want something else I can make a pit stop and get it for you," Hannibal suggested with a smile.

"Just stop and get me the Crown," Andrea stated, gaining a renewed feeling of energy.

Minutes later, Hannibal pulled into a *QuikTrip* parking lot. He wanted to make Andrea comfortable so he walked into the store and purchased a bag of chips, some blunts, a big of ice, a six pack of Coke, and a small cooler. He returned to the car and retrieved the bottle of Crown Royal from the trunk, and then sat the rest of the stuff he had bought on the floor in the backseat. He jumped into the driver's seat of his car and handed Andrea two cups of ice and the Crown Royal with a smile.

"Do you need anything else?" Hannibal asked as he rolled himself a blunt.

"I can't have the other thing I want right now," Andrea replied with wink of her eye while rubbing her hand on Hannibal's thigh.

"True, but I'm worth the wait," Hannibal said with a smile as he began to feel a slight hard form.

Back on the highway, while Hannibal was puffing on his blunt, he looked over and noticed that Andrea was pouring herself a second cup of Crown Royal. He knew she was going to feeling a little tipsy and he also figured that would bring the freak in her out. He decided to place the car on cruise control and let her have her way with him.

Andrea took a big gulp of her drink, and then whispered in his ear, "Damn, Hannibal, I want to fuck your brains out."

Those words sent a flow of hot, passionate blood to his penis, causing a full-blown hard-on. He lustfully smiled at her, thinking about how he was going to be fucking her back out in less than three hours.

"Baby, where are we going?" Andrea inquired as she began to rub on his fully swollen dick through his pants.

Andrea made a mental note to remember every word that she got out of him.

"To my house in Houston," Hannibal replied as he leaned back in his seat, feeling extreme pleasure.

Then within a split-second Andrea unzipped Hannibal's pants, removed his dick, and began sucking on it.

"Oh shit, baby! That shit feels so good!" Hannibal exclaimed. "Damn, baby, you serious with that shit, but I need you to stop before we have an accident. We only have three more hours, and believe me I'm going to give you what you want," Hannibal pleaded as he sped down the highway.

"Alright, I'll stop for now, but you better be ready to put in work because I am horny as hell," Andrea warned him with a lustful smile as she stuck his dick back in his pants.

Andrea then took Hannibal's hand and stuck it under her skirt, allowing him to feel the wetness of her pussy.

"Damn, you wetter than a mutha'fucka," Hannibal confirmed.

Ring! Ring! Ring!

Hannibal's cell phone began to ring, breaking Andrea and Hannibal's sexual, freaky thoughts. Hannibal removed his hand from under her skirt, and then he hit the speaker button on his cell phone before licking her juices from his fingers.

"Hello," Hannibal answered in a slightly irritated tone.

"Hey, cuz, what's up?" Lamar asked as he stood at the bar of the *Player's Club*.

Lamar was keeping an eye on Keisha as she was talking with an older man that looked as if he was trying to look like a pimp.

"Ain't shit. Why? What's up?" Hannibal asked as he took note of the loud music in the background.

"Check this shit out. I'm down at the Player's Club, and Keisha walked up on me. She was telling me about some dude named Twin, and she said you were looking for him. Well, I'm looking at the nigga right now," Lamar informed Hannibal.

"Listen to me. I'm going to make a phone call and whatever you do don't let him or Keisha out of your sight. I'm going to call you right back," Hannibal stated as he ended the call.

Just then he was passing a sign that read, *Welcome to Dallas, Texas.*

"I got it covered," Lamar confirmed, and then he ended the call.

Hannibal made a sharp right turn into the next rest stop, hopped out the car, and headed towards a payphone. He did not want to discuss this matter over a cell phone. Andrea simply sat in the car quietly.

"Hello! Who is this?" Dee asked, being curious as to who was calling him from a Texas number.

"Yo, Dee, this is your man Hannibal."

"Oh, what's good?" Dee asked with a sense of relief.

"Yo, I have to be quick. I got some work for you if your down but it has to be right now," Hannibal told him with a sense of urgency.

Hannibal knew that Dee lived for putting in work as long as there was a few thousand dollars on the table.

"I'm twenty-four-seven, homie," Dee said in agreement. "What's your location?" Dee asked, thinking he needed to go to Hannibal.

"Right now, I'm out of town with your little sister but the work is there," Hannibal informed him.

"Cool! Give me the four-one-one," Dee requested.

"A'ight, where you at right now?" Hannibal curiously asked.

"Right now, I was just about to go into the Player's Club to check out this honey," Dee stated as he cracked a smile.

"That shit is perfect 'cause your point man is in there as we speak," Hannibal told him with excitement. "Check this out. My cousin in there keeping an eye on the chump so I want you to hook-up with him and do you? And don't do it in the club," Hannibal instructed.

"I feel you," Dee acknowledged. "Life couldn't be easier than perfect timing. So how do I hook-up with your cousin?"

"Hold on while I make that happen," Hannibal replied before he put the payphone receiver down then grabbed his cell phone and dialed Lamar.

Ring! Ring!

"What's up, cuz?" Lamar asked as he smiled at the sight of Twin enjoying his last hours on Earth.

"Check this out. I got my man Dee on the line. Go stand by the photo booth and I am going to have him come to you."

"I'm chilling by it already while I keep an eye on this idiot," Lamar said with a laugh.

"Yo, Dee! Go inside and my cousin is by the photo booth. I'm going to stay on the phone until y'all good," Hannibal stated.

Couple minutes later Dee stated, "Yo, I see a light-skinned dude on his cell phone. Is that him?"

"Yeah, you on it. His name is Lamar," Hannibal stated before he went back to the other line. "Cuz?"

"Yeah, I'm still here," Lamar said as glanced through the crowd.

"A'ight, my man is about to walk up to you right now," Hannibal stated as anticipated the hook-up.

"A'ight, hold on. He's right here!" Lamar stated, locking eyes with Dee as he walked up to him.

"Alright, his name is Dee. All you need to do is point him in the right direction and he will handle the rest. Remember, you don't get involved," Hannibal reminded him.

"A'ight, cuz! We got this! I will holla at you later," Lamar stated as he ended the call and tapped knuckles the Dee.

"Yo, Dee, my cousin will point you in the right direction. I will see you with the stacks once I get back in town," Hannibal stated.

"Fo'sho, homie. I got you," Dee said before he ended the call, knowing it was time to handle business.

As Dee was committing his first hit, Wind was also hitting the final person on his list. He had let a week pass since he killed J-Rock. Wind decided to have a little fun and make this killing especially biblical before he returned to Hugo for the last time. He always liked to look into the eyes of those he killed so he decided to kidnap and torture his final victim.

THREE

Boom! Boom! Boom!

"Open up! This the police!" a tall, half-bald, pale-skinned, white cop yelled, while holding a shotgun over his shoulder.

The cop motioned with his free hand, instructing his partner to circle the house in order to cover the back.

"Hold-on! I'm getting dressed!" Keisha nervously shouted as she jumped out of bed.

She quickly put on a pair of jeans and a T-shirt, and then she walked to the door, wondering why the police was banging on her door at seven o'clock in the morning.

"Yeah, what's going on?" Keisha asked as she opened the door, noticing a crazy looking officer holding a shotgun.

"Keisha Jones, I'm Detective Hightower and I would like to ask you several questions about a double murder that took place around here several days ago," Detective Hightower said with a smile as he held up his badge to calm the fear in Keisha's eyes.

"Sir, I don't know anything about a murder," Keisha stated, hoping that the detective would believe her statement and leave without questioning her further.

"Well, according to our source you saw the entire ordeal and you have knowledge of who did the shooting," Detective Hightower stated as he stared her in the eyes. "Now would you like to rephrase your original statement? Before you answer that question I need to notify my partner of my status, and then I would like to come inside and speak to you further or would you prefer that we leave and come back with a warrant?"

"No, go do what you need to do then you are free to come in," Keisha stated with a frown.

Detective Hightower walked away and then came back with his partner Detective Livingston. The two detectives took seats on the couch while Keisha took a seat in the chair across from them.

"Keisha, to speak freely, I know you are protecting the shooters but if I was you I would think about myself 'cause right now you could be charged as an accessory to first degree murder," Detective Hightower explained.

"Detective Hightower, again I am telling you I don't know what you are talking about," Keisha responded, playing dumbfounded about any murder.

"Is that so?" Detective Livingston interjected for the first time. "Well, did you know Marlo Taylor and Monk Williams that lived right up the street from you?"

"Yeah, I've seen them around sometimes, but I really didn't know them," Keisha responded.

She thought it was best to admit to knowing who they are, being that they were well-known drug dealers in the town.

"Now we're getting somewhere!" Detective Hightower smiled, relaxing his demeanor a little bit. "So where were you the day they got killed."

"I was in here watching TV?" Keisha replied, remembering that Twin had told her his brother's girlfriend had said she was outside.

"Ms. Jones, do you know a guy named Alex Whibley that goes by the name of Twin?" Detective

Livingston asked, changing the subject as he removed a hand-held recorder from his pocket and placed on the coffee table.

"Not really. I've seen him around but I don't know him. Why?" Keisha nervously asked, drifting back to how she had tricked Twin into going outside just before he fell into the hands of Dee and death.

"Well, Ms. Jones, according to this recording y'all knew each other quite well!" Detective Hightower shouted as he hit play on his recorder.

"Detective Hightower, this is Twin and I'm at the Player's Club with Keisha Jones. That's the girl that my lil' brother's girlfriend said saw the entire murder. Anyway, I was just told by her that a group of guys from the Northside of Tulsa did the killing and one of the dudes is named-Oh shit!"

Pop! Pop! Pop!

"That's right, Keisha, someone shot Twin in the head three times before he could give us a name. Whoever killed him had no idea about the recorder and we found it in his pocket. Now, would you know anything about the person he was just about to name because right now your name is the only one we have, and I know you know more than what you're saying."

"No sir, I don't know anything. I'm telling you everything I know," Keisha replied in the most convincing tone she could muster.

"Ms. Jones, I'm tired of playing games with your ass! We can either do this the easy way or we can do it the hard way. I could first start with arresting you and charging you as an accessory to first degree murder that's the hard way," Detective Livingston said as he looked Keisha directly in her eyes. "Before we go that direction let's try the easy way and you give me the name of the man Twin was about to name before he was murdered."

Both the detectives hoped that Keisha would crack under the small amount of pressure and confess about the whole ordeal.

"Detective, I don't know who you're talking about!" Keisha yelled, committing to Hannibal until the end as a true ride or die chick.

"So, that's how you want to play it? Well, I'm going to give you seventy-two hours to rethink that statement and if I haven't heard from you by then I'm going to return with a warrant for your arrest," Detective Hightower forewarned as he grabbed the recorder and placed it back in his pocket. "Oh, and just so you know we are aware of your relationship with one Hannibal Watson. He's been on our radar for some time now. If he had anything to do with this and your covering for him were gonna find out. Just so you know if I do arrest you he's not gonna give a damn. He's out of town with another woman right now. You have a nice day, Ms. Jones," Detective Hightower stated with a giggle as he and Detective Livingston left.

She'll break soon, Detective Hightower thought to himself.

Keisha leaned back in her chair and cried at the thought that she was protecting a man who was out of town entertaining another woman.

*****

Down in Miami, Florida, Ace, the Widowmaker, sat on his plushed out leather recliner inside his beach front condo counting money and watching all the beautiful women strolling up and down the boardwalk.

"Life's got to be great. Look at the women I get to see every day," Ace whispered to himself with a lustful smile on his face.

"Yo, Ace, your cell phone is vibrating!" a dark-skinned guy named Guru yelled from the living room after spotting his brother's phone vibrating.

"Grab it, bro! My hands are full at this moment," Ace shouted as he continued to count his money.

"Speak," Guru bluntly answered, being curious about who was calling from out-of-state.

"Peace! Can I holla at Ace?" a dude with an anxious voice asked.

"Who is this?" Guru asked curiously, not recognizing the caller's voice, especially since they were calling from a number he didn't recognize.

"A friend of a friend," the caller replied, knowing that only Ace would know who he was immediately.

"Okay, well you hold on friend," Guru told the caller as he walked out onto the patio.

Guru told Ace what the caller had said and a huge smile came across his face.

"Yo, that's my man from the joint," Ace excitedly informed his brother as he grabbed his cell phone. "Yo, my man Twin! What's up, fool?"

"Ace, this is Cee-Lo. I'm the guy that came down with him on the last run," he explained, hoping that Ace would remember him.

Ace didn't trust anyone outside of his inner circle and Cee-Lo wasn't sure if he would be willing to talk to him.

"Oh yeah! Cee-Lo, the heavy hitter," Ace acknowledged him with a smile. "So, what's up, fam?"

Ace could sense something was wrong, being that Twin was the only one that was supposed to contact him directly.

"Well, we have a little problem. Twin was killed a week ago and the word is that some guys from Tulsa put in the work," Cee-Lo replied, knowing that Ace would avenge the death of Twin at any cost.

Ace was indebted to Twin. Twin had saved Ace's life during a prison riot while they both were still locked down.

"Damn, not my man! What kind of beef was going down and why did it take you a week for you to tell me?" Ace inquired, knowing that Twin was all about getting his money.

"He was running down some info on some punks that killed his people, Marlo and Monk. I did some digging and the same dudes found out he was asking around and they killed him too," Cee-Lo explained before he remembered that Twin mentioned a girl named Keisha being involved. "I don't know the guy's name but it's a broad named Keisha that I hear knows exactly what went down. I'm going to pay her a visit for some more info."

"Say no more, fam. I'm on it like yesterday," Ace hastily informed Cee-Lo.

"Good looking and once I know what the girl has to say I will holla at ya," Cee-Lo concluded.

Cee-Lo made a mental note that he was going to teach the girl Keisha a about fucking with the wrong crew.

"I hear you. One," Ace stated then he ended the call.

Ace reached over and grabbed the half of a blunt that was in his ashtray. He put fire to it and took several deep puffs.

He whispered to himself, “Don’t trip, homie. I gotcha.”

Ace blew smoke into the air and thought of how those that killed Twin would be dealt with at any cost.

“Guru, cancel everything for the next week ‘cause we have some personal business to attend to in Oklahoma!” Ace yelled out as he laid his head back on the chair.

Ace drifted back to two months ago, when Twin and Cee-Lo had flew down to Miami and hung out with him and his little brother Guru for the weekend. They partied like they were rock stars on South Beach with all the half-naked Spanish women. Twin and Cee-Lo had coped five kilos of cocaine and drove back to Pensacola.

“I feel you, bro! I’ve got your back!” Guru responded, knowing that it was time to forget about pleasure and strap on his game face.

*****

Three days later, back in Tulsa, Hannibal was cruising around in his Mercedes-Benz. He noticed some of the guys posted up in the parking lot at Chamberlain Park. They were holding court and regulating the drug flow on the Northside. He came to a halt at the stop sign and allowed his thoughts to drift back to when he was in Houston with Andrea. Him and her spent the entire time chilling at his new house all cuddled up in each other's arms. They always ended the night with a session of passionate lovemaking. He loved to put her in the doggy style position, open scissor, exposing her pussy.

Moments later, creeping up while Hannibal was caught up in his thoughts about his most recent sexual escapade with Andrea, a brown tinted windowed four door old Chevy Classic pulled up beside him and instantly the two windows that faced him came down. Hannibal glanced over at the car, noticing four semi-automatic weapons piercing through the windows.

Blak! Blak! Blak! Blak!

The weapons began to spit. Hannibal quickly ducked as low as he could in the car seat and he hit the gas pedal. The windows shattered and the bullets penetrated through the Mercedes-Benz, forcing him to continue to speed through traffic. He hastily grabbed cell phone, hitting the speed dial to Lamar. He was severely shook up but thankful that he was able to escape death and injury. He was now concerned about who was trying to kill him in his own backyard.

"What's up, cuz?" Lamar asked when he answered his phone on the third ring.

"Cuz, you ain't gonna believe this shit! Somebody just tried to kill me over by Chamberlain Park!" Hannibal shouted as he pulled up to his sister's apartment.

"What? You alright?" Lamar shockingly asked, knowing that war had been declared in the streets.

"Yeah I'm good. They shot my Benz up though," Hannibal stated as he stepped out of his car, noticing all the bullet holes in his car.

"Did you get a good look at the shooters?" Lamar eagerly asked, feeling the need for some revenge.

"Nah, but I know there was four of them. They were in an old Chevy Classic with dark tinted windows," Hannibal replied. "Anyway, get everybody together and have them meet up at the trap house out east at nine o'clock tonight. You feel me?"

"You know I'm down with you, but I thought you said we were done with all the shoot 'em up bang-bang bullshit," Lamar stated.

"I thought we were done with it too, but this shit is personal," Hannibal stated, feeling the urge to take it to the streets and find out who was trying to have him killed.

Hannibal knew that Twin's homies were looking for the person behind his death. He didn't worry about it that much because he figured they didn't know anything about him. He had obviously underestimated their determination.

"I'm on it, cuz. Peace," Lamar stated before he ended the call.

Lamar jumped out of his car, noticing a strange, dark tinted windowed Honda Accord cruising down the street as if it was scoping out the area. He pulled out his Glock .45 and waved it in the air as he walked to the corner of the street. He watched the Honda Accord speed off the block. Lamar knew that it was time to go to war.

Later that night, in the basement of the trap house, Hannibal walked around the room with his red nose pit-bull at his side. He was pondering over who was trying to kill him. He was extremely concerned about the fact that whoever wanted him dead was bold enough to come after him in broad daylight on his own turf. As he saw it he only had two options. He could get out of town for a while to Oklahoma City until things cooled down or he could start dropping bodies. The first order of business was to find out who gave the order to have him hit. He didn't want a long drawn out war. He knew it was bad for business. He wanted this ordeal to be over with quickly, and the only way to make that happen was to hit whoever was giving the order. If you cut of the head of the snake the body will eventually stop moving. Those were the words he lived by.

"Yo, cuz, after I hung up with you earlier I spotted a unknown Honda Accord cruising by my house as if it was casing the place out," Lamar spoke up, breaking Hannibal's pondering thoughts.

Hannibal observed all the members of Hustla'z Inc. come to attention at the mention of the unknown Honda Accord.

"Do you have any idea what that's about?" Hannibal asked curiously, convinced that something was going down behind closed doors.

"Naw, not right off hand, but I heard that the detectives been sweating your girl Keisha real hard about them murders," Lamar replied in a concerned tone of voice, knowing that sooner or later Keisha would need to be dealt with before she cracked under pressure, sending them all to prison.

"Oh yeah, she's got to be dealt with," Gunslinger chimed in.

"Yo, y'all chill out. Keisha is solid. She'll go to prison before she snitches. Plus, if she puts us in the jackpot she would be putting herself in. She's smarter than that," Hannibal hastily defended.

"I put word out on the street about that brown Chevy Classic and word got back to me that it belonged to some of Twin's people from down south," Lamar stated with a sense of concern, trying to steer the conversation away from the problem that Keisha might cause.

"Is that right? Now we're getting somewhere," Hannibal stated as he cracked a vengeful smile. "Yo, Gunslinger, do you still have your connections down south?" Hannibal inquired, thinking it was time for them to do some secret intelligence on who was running the show from down there.

"Yeah, I still have a few friends down that way," Gunslanger replied, catching the vibe on what Hannibal was trying to get at.

"Now check this out. I want you to put the word out that I'm offering twenty-five thousand dollars for the name of the guy that tried to have me killed," Hannibal stated. "Until we find out what's going on, I want everybody to tool up and be extra careful. Don't kill anybody if you don't have to, but I do want you to do whatever you have to in order to get that information."

"Consider it done, fam," Gunslanger replied with a smile, knowing that his people would do what he needed for that kind of cash.

"Lamar, I want you to holla at that redneck detective and see what kind of information he has on Twin's murder. See how close they think they are to flipping Keisha."

"I feel you, cuz. I'm on it like yesterday," Lamar responded, knowing that with a couple thousand dollars on the table Detective Rogers crooked as would provide them the information they needed.

"Bey, I want you and Murder to work the streets around here for info on who is trying to get at us. You feel me?" Hannibal asked, further instructing as he stopped at the head of the round table and took a seat.

"We on it," Bey responded attentively as he nodded his head towards Murder who also nodded his head in agreeance.

"Lastly, I need you to make all of our people at the trap houses and on the block aware of what's happening. Make sure everybody is watching their ass," Hannibal concluded as he locked eyes with each person sitting at the table. "Now, in the meantime, I'm gonna pay little Ms. Keisha a visit. You feel me?"

They all stood from the table and prepared to leave so that each of them could go take care of their business.

FOUR

Smack! Smack!

"Bitch, I'm gonna ask you one more time, who pulled the hit on Marlo and Monk!" Cee-Lo yelled, grabbing Keisha by her hair and slapping her across the face twice for the third time.

"Please stop!" Keisha screamed out as she balled up on the floor. "I told you, I don't know!" Keisha pleaded as tears rolled down her face and blood dripped from her nose and lip.

"Dave, grab this bitch and bring her into the bedroom!" Cee-Lo angrily ordered as he started to put on his black leather gloves, thinking it was time to try a different approach in order to get Keisha to talk.

"No!" Keisha yelled as Dave dragged her into the bedroom by her ankles, instantly noticing the other intruder was holding a stun gun in his hand.

Pop!

Keisha's world turned black after being hit in the face by Cee-Lo again, however this he hit her with a closed fist. When she woke up, she was stripped naked and tied to her bed posts with all four of her limbs spread apart. The two intruders hovered over her with evil grins, holding stun guns in their hands.

"I'm glad to see you've decided to rejoin us," Cee-Lo remarked as he walked closer to the bed, playing with the volts on the stun gun.

"Please don't hurt me anymore!" Keisha cried out, pleading for her life.

"If you don't want to get hurt give me what I came for," Cee-Lo responded with a smile. "I don't want to hurt you, but you will talk or you will die."

"I told you I don't know who he is," Keisha replied as tears continued to flow from her eyes.

"Wrong answer!" Cee-Lo yelled before he hit Keisha with the stun gun.

Pain ripped through Keisha's body. She felt as if she had accidentally touched as steaming hot iron.

"Please stop!" Keisha pleaded, feeling her breathing getting low at the thought of being hit by the stun gun again.

"I'll stop once you give me the information I need. It's him that I want not you. There's no reason for you to get hurt or die because of this," Cee-Lo stated as a wicked grin spread across his face. "I'm listening."

"I'm telling you I really don't know!" Keisha replied, begging in thought that God would make her intruder stop.

"Wrong answer, ma! This isn't going to end well for you," Cee-Lo grinned, and then he stuck the stun gun to Keisha's thigh about an inch from her vagina.

Cee-Lo sent fifty thousand volts surging through Keisha's body, causing her to scream out in pain. She urinated on herself as she loss total control of her bodily functions.

"Stop! Please stop! I'll tell you what you want to know!" Keisha moaned as the pain constantly penetrated her body at the thought of the stun gun shocking her body again.

"Now that's a good girl," Cee-Lo stated as he cracked a devilish grin and leaned in closer to Keisha's mouth, waiting for her to confess. "I'm listening."

"It was Hannibal Watson and his crew," Keisha whispered, convinced that her strength had been broken.

"See that wasn't that hard. Thank you," Cee-Lo smiled as he rubbed the tears from Keisha's eyes. "Dave, end this bitch," Cee-Lo instructed, feeling absolutely no remorse for Keisha as he walked out of the bedroom, satisfied with his work. "Now it's time to deal with this nigga Hannibal and his punk ass crew."

Dave stood over Keisha with a .38 snug nose tucked into a pillow. He positioned the pillow over Keisha's face and pulled the trigger, sending her brains flying out the back of her skull.

"Yeah, bitch! You was down with the wrong niggas," Dave whispered under his breath as he walked out of Keisha's bedroom to join Cee-Lo with a smile on his face. "That's a rap!"

They walked out of her house just like a couple thieves in the night, committed to finding Hannibal Watson and his crew to take their revenge game to the next level.

*****

Meanwhile, back in Tulsa inside *Cloud Nine Strip Club,* Hannibal was downing his third Heineken as he watched several young tenders do their thing while his mind replayed the shooting that nearly took his life over-and-over again.

"Man, there has got to be an explanation for all of this," Hannibal whispered to himself as his thoughts drifted to Keisha and whether she would remain loyal to him and continue to hold up under pressure. "I've got to go see her and make sure she has her head together."

Hannibal stood up from the bar, downed the remainder of his beer, and then reached in his pocket to leave the waitress a tip.

"Leaving so soon?" Detective Rogers asked as he approached Hannibal at the bar with a cunning smile on his face.

"Time is money. Don't you understand that?" Hannibal replied, noticing the smile on Detective Rogers' face.

"I think I have some useful information for you," Detective Rogers replied.

"What the hell. I guess I can stay for a while," Hannibal stated, catching the vibe that the detective wanted to talk.

"I think that would serve you best," Detective Rogers said, showing his coffee stained smile.

"Is that so?" Hannibal remarked with a smile of his own. "Well, can I get you a beer?"

"Sure, I'll take one of those Heineken's," Detective Rogers said as he took a seat.

"So, detective, what's good?" Hannibal eagerly asked after ordering both of them another beer.

"A murder contract that's what good," Detective Rogers bluntly replied.

"Oh yeah! That not good," Hannibal commented with a sly grin as he reached in his pocket, peeled off a thousand dollars from his money roll, and then dropped on the ground between the two the two of them. "Damn, detective, did you drop something?"

Hannibal pointed at the money that was on the ground.

"Hmm, that looks very nice," Detective Rogers stated before he bent down and picked up the money off the floor then stuffed it into his pocket. "Word around town is that you ordered the hit on Marlo and Monk in Muskogee over some petty bullshit turf beef. The word is that you also have a big problem coming your way."

"I'm still listening, detective," Hannibal restated, noticing the confused look on Detective Rogers' face.

"There is one big problem. We're trying to rundown a witness that will tell us who the killers are and who the leader is. We're working with Muskogee police but we're taking the lead on this shit because our intelligence tells us the leader is from Tulsa. This shit isn't going to just go away," Detective Rogers informed, not giving a damn about jeopardizing his job and the investigation.

Detective Rogers grabbed his beer and took a huge gulp, and then another smile spread across his face.

"So, detective, are you asking if I hired a group of people to go and kill Marlo and Monk over some type of street beef?" Hannibal asked, committed to keeping Detective Rogers in the dark about his personal involvement in the murders.

"I said you led the group but if you want to put it that way, yep that pretty much sums it up until the investigation is completed," Detective Rogers stated as he took another huge gulp of his beer.

"Well, detective, for the record I didn't order or lead any group of men to commit a murder on no one, so you and your department need to reevaluate your info," Hannibal stated confidently because the information given to him told him he still had time to eliminate the threat.

"Oh, don't worry my man! By the time we get done working that girl that we think saw the whole damn thing we will have everything we need," Detective Rogers boasted as he downed the last of his beer and gave Hannibal a slick smirk. "Oh yeah, we know about that bitch and we know you been fuckin' her too. I hear she's a tough little bitch. We didn't break her on the first try but we're going back."

"Well, good for y'all, but I guess that's bad for her, huh?" Hannibal asked. *Damn, I guess Keisha has got to go,* Hannibal thought to himself. "Well, detective, it's been nice chatting with you. You stay in touch because that just might be to your advantage. You feel me?" Hannibal stated as he placed a fifty-dollar bill on the bar then Hannibal motioned for the bartender to serve Detective Rogers another beer. "Darling, keep the change and make sure this ole mutha'fucka here makes it home safe," Hannibal addressed the white half-naked bartender as he pointed his finger at Detective Rogers. "Peace!"

Hannibal threw up two finger with a smile as he walked off to go pay Keisha a farewell visit.

*****

Thirty minutes later with murder on his mind, Hannibal pulled up in front of Keisha's house. He instantly noticed that her front door was wide open but all the lights inside the house were out.

"Damn, this shit don't look right," Hannibal whispered to himself.

He put the car in park but left it running so that he could make a quick getaway if necessary.

"Damn, this game got me twisted," Hannibal said to himself as he reached in his glove compartment to get his .40 caliber Desert Eagle.

He tip-toed in the dark to do what needed to be done even though in his heart he felt that Keisha wouldn't cross him even in the face of death. After Hannibal eased up to Keisha's front door, he called out to her in a low tone of voice. He again got a feeling that something just wasn't right, being that the house was extremely quiet with no sign of anyone being present. With constant suspicion, Hannibal tip-toed into Keisha's house, observing that the living room was out of order and it looked as if there had been a scuffle. He pulled out his gun as he continued to walk through the house, heading towards Keisha's bedroom. Hannibal was prepared to blast off hot slugs if an unexpected intruder headed towards him.

"Damn!" Hannibal shouted as he stepped into Keisha's bedroom, spotting her tied to her bedpost with her brains blown out.

Instantly tears came to his eyes, and he wondered who in the hell had done such a viscous thing to his ride or die chick.

"Damn, this shit's gotten too fucking crazy!" Hannibal shouted as he ran his hand across his face.

Fool, you're in a dead woman's crib, Hannibal thought as he snapped out of his mental daze. He knew he needed to get out of there as soon as possible before someone popped up and thought he was the killer. With sympathy, Hannibal covered Keisha's body, and then he dialed 911 to inform them that a dead body was on the scene. He quickly tip-toed out of Keisha's house, puzzled over who could have possibly beat him to the punch of eliminating Keisha. He also wondered what information Keisha may have given up before she took her last breath.

"Damn, I hope babygirl died being one hundred," Hannibal mumbled as he hopped into his Mercedes-Benz and drove away from Keisha's house.

Hannibal lit a blunt of sticky-icky green and replayed the entire bloody scene in his head over-and-over again.

*****

A few hours later across town at the Ramada Inn, Detective Rogers paced the hotel room back and forth, venting at the thought of Cee-Lo killing their only witness instead of just scaring the information out of her that they both were desperate in need to know. He wanted a positive ID on the person who was determined to eliminate anybody that was standing in his way of controlling the streets.

"Where's this mutha'fucka? I'm going to kick his ass myself!" Detective Rogers angrily shouted as he continued to pace the hotel room, waiting for Cee-Lo to return back to the hotel room with his money.

Knock! Knock! Knock!

Cee-Lo banged on the hotel room door, and then listened as he heard someone hastily running towards it.

"Yeah, who is it?" Detective Rogers asked as he looked through the peephole.

"It's me! Who else would it be asshole!" Cee-Lo replied in laughter, knowing that Detective Rogers was a sucker for a little bit of cash and would sellout his mother for a little bit of nothing.

"'Bout funkin' time!" Detective Rogers shouted as he opened the hotel room door, allowing Cee-Lo to walk in. "Hey, you fuckin' asshole! Who the fuck told you that it was ok to go and kill the fuckin' girl?" Detective Rogers barked as he grabbed Cee-Lo by the shirt and slammed him against the wall.

Detective Rogers stared at him with deadly, killer eyes.

"First of all, you better get your fuckin' hands off of me you crooked ass mutha'fuckin' cop!" Cee-Lo angrily demanded, staring eye-to-eye with Detective Rogers.

"If I don't what are you going to do, you fuckin' piece of shit?" Detective Rogers replied angrily as he returned Cee-Lo's evil stare. "That's what I thought!" Detective Roger commented as he released Cee-Lo from his grip. "Now, tell me what the fuck happened!" Detective Rogers stated as he stepped out of Cee-Lo's way.

Detective Rogers observed Cee-Lo closely as he straightened out his clothes to make sure he did that instead of pulling out his gun.

"Man, the bitch wouldn't cooperate so I told my man to deal with her ass. I didn't tell the mutha'fucka to kill the bitch, but fuck it the bitch is dead now," Cee-Lo stated with a straight face, lying and reaching to turn on the tape recorder that he had in his pocket.

Cee-Lo wanted to cover his bases and make sure that he had just as much dirt on Detective Rogers as he had on him.

"So, did she give you any information on the murders?" Detective Rogers curiously asked, hoping that

Cee-Lo had at least gotten Keisha to give up the name of the leader.

Detective Rogers was nervous about having this whole thing over because he was caught in the middle of it all due to his greed.

"Hell no! That bitch kept saying that she didn't know nothin'," Cee-Lo stated, thinking he had a better solution for Hannibal then letting the system put him in jail for killing Twin. "Anyway, detective, I thought you said she was y'all number one witness."

Cee-Lo stared at Detective Rogers with a deceivingly confused look on his face. Cee-Lo was trying to get Detective Rogers to reveal more valuable information to make sure that he was covering all areas of eliminating anybody connected to the killing of his homie Twin.

"Fuck all that! Where's my money!" Detective Rogers shouted, breaking out of his daze of twisted thoughts about Cee-Lo trying to play him like a fool.

"Man, I shouldn't even give you this shit 'cause the bitch didn't even tell us shit, but to keep it real I'm goin' honor my word so that we can continue to do business in the future. You feel me?" Cee-Lo responded with a grin as he reached in his pocket and pulled out five thousand dollars that was rubber band together. "Now, before I give you this money I want to know what Twin said on your voicemail about that bitch?"

"First of all, who said anything about Twin leaving a message on my phone in the first place? I'm getting a little tired of your shit," Detective Rogers stated, assuming that someone on the force was also playing both sides of the game.

"That shit don't matter! You just need to answer my fucking questions! I'm getting tired of your shit too! You need to understand one thing Detective Rogers. I will have no problem with making you a cadaverous mutha'fucka so don't think about lying to me. I know more than you think I do," Cee-Lo warned as he waved the money in Detective Rogers' face. "Now you need to start talking."

Cee-Lo knew that it would only take a minute before Detective Rogers would start to confess his soul. He could never turn down an easy payday.

"This is what he said mutha'fucka!" Detective Rogers shouted before he pulled out his .45 caliber automatic with a silencer attached to it.

Cee-Lo stood his ground confidently, and stated, "I'm listening. You redneck mutha'fucka. Does the cat got yo' tongue or do I need to help you find yo' way?" Cee-Lo taunted as he continued to wave the money in Detective Rogers' face.

Detective Rogers hesitated and seriously thought about simply killing Cee-Lo and taking the money but he reconsidered because he didn't know who Cee-Lo was working for, and he didn't want to be looking over his shoulder any more than he already was.

"Alright mutha'fucka! The recording said that Twin was looking for one guy from Tulsa that headed up the crew that killed Marlo and Monk," Detective Rogers stated, feeling as if he was giving up too much information. "Now give me my mutha'fuckin' money!" Detective Rogers shouted as he stepped closer to Cee-Lo and snatched the money out of his hand.

"I've had all the bullshit I'ma take off of you, detective. Police or no police, you need to watch your fuckin' mouth. Now, it's been nice doing business with you, bastard," Cee-Lo stated as he reached in his shirt pocket for a Cuban cigar. "When you get more information, you get at me and don't you spend all that money in one place. So, until we meet again I'll holla at chu'," Cee-Lo stated with a slight giggle.

Cee-Lo walked towards the door, and thought to himself, *I'm gonna let you live a little while longer then I'm gonna bury your redneck ass.*

"Whatever you mutha'fucka. Next time don't do shit without my ok, and keep me posted on any new developments," Detective Rogers responded as he followed Cee-Lo out of the hotel room door.

Little did Detective Rogers know, but Cee-Lo was serious about not taking any more insults from him.

Yeah, when this shit is all you're gonna here from me is the sound of a bullet as it pierces your mutha'fuckin' skull, Detective Rogers thought to himself.

As Detective Rogers walked to his car, he placed the money to his nose and took a big breath. He envisioned himself at the tables in Las Vegas very shortly. Once he reached his car door, he turned around to find Cee-Lo standing behind him with his gun pointed to his face. Cee-Lo let off one shot that caught Detective Rogers between the eyes. Detective Rogers slumped over and fell on top of Cee-Lo. Cee-Lo opened the car door and placed Detective

Rogers' dead body behind in the driver's seat. He reached into Detective Rogers' pocket and took back the five thousand dollars he had given him, closed the car, and then he wiped the car handle off to remove any fingerprints that he may have left.

I told you to shut up your mutha'fuckin' mouth, Cee-Lo thought to himself as he walked to his car.

Since people couldn't see inside of the vehicle due to the dark tint on the car, Detective Rogers body was not discovered until a hotel guest complained to the staff about the smell coming from the car five days later. Detectives Jenkins and Finley were assigned to the case. The cheap hotel didn't have any surveillance on the parking lot and there were no eye witnesses so the case went cold. Everyone in the department, including the detectives that were assigned the case, thought Detective Rogers was dirty or washed up so they didn't make too much of a fuss when they were unable to solve the case.

FIVE

Hannibal slammed the door to his condo in Oklahoma City and threw his keys on the coffee table. He slumped down onto his recliner and thought about the life that he lived and if it was all worth it if his friends and family had to die. He actually liked Keisha but she was a casualty of war and that part he hated.

Hannibal thought about his new home in Houston, Texas and possibly building a life with Andrea. He put those thoughts out of his mind as he grabbed the remote to turn on the ten o'clock news.

"Today we regret to report yet another gangland style killing. The killing was recorded and sent to our office but it's too graphic for viewing. I can say that I have never seen anything like this before," the newscaster stated before they went to a commercial.

Hannibal knew who did the hit and why. He knew it was time to settle his affairs with the hitman Wind.

Inside Hannibal's closet Dee was waiting. He was crunched down and waiting for Hannibal to walk in the room.

As Hannibal entered the room Dee jumped out, and asked, "What's up?"

"Man, I must be trippin'," Hannibal mumbled to himself as he eased into his bedroom, noticing that everything was untouched and just as he had left it.

"Say bruh, you have a real big problem," Dee warned as he approached Hannibal.

"Man, I am glad to see you, but how in the fuck did you get in my condo?"

"Look, I came to give you the heads up on something. There is a hit out, and I think it has something to do with you," Dee stated as he walked and took a seat on the chair in the corner of the room.

"What? Who is the mutha'fucka that wants me dead?"

"You clipped a couple guys a while back. Those guys had big connections," Dee stated, thinking about his loyalty to a friend and a huge payday.

"I don't know shit about that, but I need to know who is coming at me," Hannibal said as he took a seat on the bed.

"The word is that the people are coming from somewhere down south. That is all I know. You need to tighten up 'cause if I can get at you in your bedroom, you can best believe they can."

"I want to know something. How much are they putting out there?" Hannibal asked curiously.

"I don't know, but I would say you have a big problem that needs to be dealt with. These niggas ain't gonna let up until they think the score has been settled. I'ma put my ear to the street and find out what I can."

"Do what you can and keep me posted. I will deal with this shit myself."

*****

Click!

Hannibal quickly hit the kitchen light switch, turning on his overhead light. He instantly spotted two intruders dressed in all black gear peeking into his window, and then in the blink of an eye they took off running at the sight of Hannibal raising his gun towards them. He halted before firing and immediately took off running towards his back door. He kept an eye on the intruders as they hauled ass towards the end of the street where they quickly jumped into a black four-door Chevy Blazer and sped off. Hannibal made it to the curb and blasted off four shots at the truck.

Blak! Blak! Blak! Blak!

He missed the truck as it went just out of range.

"Boy, it's on now! You mutha'fucka's have me fucked up. All this bullshit over two punks. This shit has to be about somethin' else. I have to figure this out right now," Hannibal angrily whispered under his breath as he stood in the middle of the street.

He looked down the empty street while he held his gun down to his side, noticing several lights come on at his neighbor's house. Given the fact that he was in Houston, Texas and the only person that knew of the location of his house was Andrea he immediately became suspicious of her and her intentions.

With the thought of getting out the sight of his nosey neighbors, Hannibal stuffed his gun inside of his waistband and began to walk back to his house, convinced that it was time for him to take the first moving flight out of Houston and head back to Tulsa, Oklahoma.

SIX

"Girl, you almost got us killed!" Rita screamed out in a fearful tone as she sat down on the bed at the hotel and stared at Andrea who was in deep thought about the situation that they were in. "Girl, I thought you said that Hannibal was out of town!" Rita frowned, wondering what Andrea was thinking about so hard, being that she was completely quiet all the way to the hotel.

"I did think he was out of town. At least that is what his people told me," Andrea broke her silence, thinking that killing Hannibal was going to be harder then she anticipated.

"Anyway, girl, what's up with you trying to creep into Hannibal's crib all about?" Rita asked, knowing thinking that Andrea's reasoning was all about trying to find out where Hannibal kept his drug stash then trying to rob him blind.

Rita wanted revenge for the way he treated her in the past when it came to her ex-boyfriend Ced.

"Bitch, you asking to many questions. Why don't you just shut the fuck up!" Andrea bluntly replied, giving Rita a nasty look. "Now stay in your place 'cause I'm running this show."

"Oh, is that so?" Rita asked sarcastically, staring at Rita with a bitchy attitude. "Well, your ass didn't say that when you asked me to holla at Angel to find out when Hannibal and his cousin were going back to Atlantic City so your nasty ass could be there to hook up with him like your ass just happened to be there by coincidence," Rita continued to babble off at the mouth, getting into her feelings towards the way Andrea was treating her.

Smack!

"Bitch, watch your funkin' mouth!" Andrea angrily shouted before she slapped Rita across her face as she pulled out her chrome 9 mm handgun and stuck it in Rita's face. "Now, bitch, do you have somethin' else to say out that filthy ass mouth of yours?"

Andrea stood in front of Rita, watching her holding her face in her hands as a tear rolled down her cheek.

"Answer me, bitch!" Andrea screamed.

"Nah, I ain't got nothin' to say, but you didn't have to slap me," Rita sobbed, looking up at Andrea like a little child who had just been disciplined for doing something wrong.

"Anyway, bitch, you don't have no idea what this shit between me and Hannibal is about. Frankly, it's none of your damn business. You hear me?" Andrea stressed in her daddy-Mack tone of voice, feeling her pussy getting wet at the sight of Rita being totally submissive to her.

"Yeah, I hear you. I'm sorry," Rita replied softly before she put her arms around Andrea's waist.

She began to unbuckle Andrea's jeans, allowing them to fall to her ankles. She also removed Andrea's white cotton panties. Andrea stepped her feet out of her jeans and panties, leaving her completely naked from the waist down with her nipples poking through her shirt. Then Rita pulled Andrea quickly, snatching her down one bed, while she hurriedly removed her own jeans and panties. Rita spread Andrea's legs apart and began to suck on her clitoris, removing all the anger and anxiety from Andrea's mind by the sound of her moans.

"Oh, that feels too good! Just like that!" Andrea screamed in ecstasy as she rotated her hips. "Bitch, suck that clit harder! This pussy is about to cum!"

Rita took Andera's clit in her mouth and sucked as hard as she possible could, while thrusting three fingers deep into her dripping wet pussy.

Rita hit Andrea's G-spot, and listened to her moan, "Oh, bitch!"

Andrea's body wiggled, twisted, and then relaxed as the flow of her sweet juices made their way down Rita's throat. Rita continued to suck on Andrea's pussy until she was sure that Andrea was fully satisfied.

"Bitch, who you love now?" Rita asked as she continued to finger fuck Andrea's pussy, while teasing her hard, numb nipples.

"You Rita!" Andrea moaned as she felt herself about to climax again. "Oh, bitch, this pussy is cumming again!" Andrea screamed out, causing Rita to push harder and deeper into her pussy at a fast pace.

This sent Andrea into a sexual induced frenzy as her pussy burned with intense heat. Then with a sudden halt, Rita positioned herself over Andrea in the sixty-nine position, allowing both of them to suck and bite on each other's clitoris as they finger fucked one another. Their sexual escapade ended with them laying in the same position with an uncontrollable bond to each other.

"I love you, Andrea," Rita whispered, removing herself from on top of Andrea to lay upon her swollen breast.

"I love you too, bitch," Andrea responded, allowing her thoughts to hastily drift to the matter at hand and consider her next move in order to carry out the hit on Hannibal.

*****

That following Thursday afternoon at around one p.m., Hannibal pulled out of his driveway, dialing his realtor Kenya Grayson on the phone. He was convinced that he could no longer trust living there since someone had breached his security. To him security was priority one, especially since he had become a million-dollar figure in the hustle game.

"BlueShield Realtors, how may I direct your call?" a professional voiced female asked, answering the phone on the second ring.

"Yes, may I speak to Mrs. Grayson please?" Hannibal asked politely, stopping at the entrance/exit gate to his house and taking one last look at the luxury house that he had fought so hard to get.

"Hold please," the professional voiced female instructed, hitting her call center button, sending soft Jazz melodies playing in Hannibal's ears, allowing him to further ponder over the two unknown intruders.

"Hello, this is Kenya Grayson. Your dream home doesn't have to stay that way, and I'm here to make it all come true," Mrs. Grayson stated, routinely carrying out her catch a client line. "Now, how can I help you?"

"Yes, Mrs. Grayson, this is Hannibal Watson. Do you remember me?"

"Sure, how can I help you, Mr. Watson?" Mrs. Grayson asked convincingly as she searched through her files on her laptop to retrieve Hannibal's buyer's information so that she knew exactly who she was talking too.

"Yes, I would like to place my house back on the market as soon as possible," Hannibal informed her, knowing that Mrs. Grayson was going to be pleased being that she felt forced to sell the luxury home to a young black man in the middle of an all-white neighborhood.

She sold the house even in the midst of all the negative insults and complaints from the rich, white people of the neighborhood because it was a cash deal and a quick payday.

"May I ask why, Mr. Watson?" Mrs. Grayson inquired, trying to give Hannibal the impression that she was concerned as to why he would be willing to place the house back on the market after only owning it for less than a year.

"I have no use for the house, and I would like to move forward," Hannibal stated, telling a straightforward lie, while pondering over the thought of who could have given up the location of his secret hideout.

Only his cousin Lamar and his newfound favorite girl Andrea knew about his house down in Houston. That house was intended to be a place where he could go to get away from all the drama that came with the hustle game but still it followed him like a bad cold.

"Well, in that case, Mr. Watson, I will respect your wishes and have someone go out there to lock the place up," Mrs. Grayson responded as she jacked her arms in the air in celebration.

She never wanted to sale a house in that neighborhood to a young black man. Her mind drifted to her plan to have an unknowing rich buyer make an overpriced bid of five hundred thousand dollars in order to be able to force Hannibal to sale. She was doing this, knowing that the house was only worth three hundred and seventy-five thousand.

"Mrs. Grayson, as for my furniture and other belongings, could you please have someone pack them up and store them for me until I am able to send a crew to retrieve them," Hannibal inquired.

"Sure, Mr. Watson, I'll take care of everything," Mrs. Grayson agreed with enthusiasm.

"Thanks again, Mrs. Grayson, and it's been nice doing business with you," Hannibal said as he pulled out of view of the house and headed towards the interstate.

"Likewise, Mr. Watson," Mrs. Grayson stated politely, cracking a smile as she thought of the huge profit she was going to turn on the house now that Hannibal was out of the picture.

Mrs. Grayson planned to sale the house at the overinflated price, and then give Hannibal a story of how she was only able to get three hundred thousand dollars for it due to the current market. She would then pocket the rest for herself including her usual commission.

"Have a great day, Mr. Watson. You're in good hands as always," Mrs. Grayson assured him before she ended the call.

Hannibal was heading west to Baton Rouge, Louisiana to meet up with a guy he had been buying product from at a discount every now and then that they called Burna. As he sped down the highway, he dialed Burna's cell phone to give him the heads up that he was heading his way for some urgent business.

"Fuck with me," Burna yelled into the cell phone when he answered.

"What's up, Burna? You still out there gettin' that paper?" Hannibal asked with a slight giggle, knowing his man Burna was serious about getting money and counting it down to the last penny.

"Ain't no other way to live if you ask me. What's good in your hood?" Burna asked, feeling himself in a big way.

"Same shit different day. You know how it goes."

"Yeah I do. So, what's really going on with you, Hannibal? It seems kind of funny that you would be callin' me this time of year. It's not even close to Mardi Gras and I know it's not dead up there in Oklahoma as far as supply, so to what do I owe this phone call?"

Burna only expected a call when supply was tight or during Mardi Gras season when he would join Hannibal to chill out on Bourbon Street, catch a parade or two, and then Hannibal would cope a couple of birds before leaving town. He knew Hannibal to be a good businessman and a friend, but he knew something had to be going on for him to be calling out of nowhere.

"This isn't a pleasure call. It is a little bit of an emergency, but I would rather not have this discussion on the phone so I'm heading your direction as we speak."

Hannibal was hoping that Burna would catch his drift and not press the issue any further until they were face-to-face.

"Say no more, fam. I'm closing down shop right now, and I will be ready to meet with you here shortly. So, when are you gettin' into town, playboy?" Burna asked, suspecting that Hannibal had some serious business on his mind.

"Most likely within the next two hours since I'm already motoring down the highway right now," Hannibal replied.

"Perfect! Just hit me on my cell as soon as you get into town. I'll have someone come meet you and you can follow them from there," Burna stated as he took a look at his diamond bezel Rolex watch, making a mental note of what time he needed to be ready.

"Good looking, fam. I'll owe you one," Hannibal acknowledged as he sat back in his seat and allowed to the cool air coming through the window to soothe him.

"Not in this lifetime or the next 'cause you my man and I'm down wit'chu. You feel me?" Burna asked, remembering how Hannibal was there for him when he was robbed of his whole shipment and had absolutely no product.

Hannibal fronted Burna what he needed to get back on his feet and helped him to track down the guys that robbed him.

"In a minute," Hannibal stated, and then he hit the end button on his cell phone.

*****

Down in the basement of an abandoned house right off of Boston in Tulsa, Murder sat tied up on a chair. He had been sitting on that chair butt-naked all night. He was soaked from head to toe in hot honey. He feared what his enemies were planning, being that they were constantly covering his naked body with the hot, sticky substance. He hated the fact that he had allowed his dick to cause him to fall for the sexual teasing of a red-boned female with a phat ass who promised to suck and fuck his brains out. She enticed him back to her place and that is when he fell into his enemy's hands. The burning became so intense that it caused him to drift in and out of consciousness.

"Yo, homie, you still with us?" Slick asked, slapping Murder upside the head as he stepped in front of him, raising his chin with his finger then removing it. "Damn, y'all done killed the mutha'fucka!"

"Don't trip! I got somethin' to wake his black ass up," Dolla spoke up, walking into the basement carrying another hot bowl of honey.

"Ahh!" Murder screamed out as Dolla poured some of the hot honey in between his legs, causing him to come back to life due to the intense pain.

"Well, look who decided to rejoin the party," Dolla remarked in laughter as he stepped up into Murder's face with a devilish grin. "Now, are you ready to tell me what I want to hear?"

"Oh, ok!" Murder said with a moan, raising his head up and noticing grins on everybody's face except for his cousin, Dave, who was regretting being a part of abducting him for what was supposed to be for information purposes only.

"Good! Now tell me who your leader is and what is the name of your group."

"Your mama!" Murder replied, cracking a small grin, knowing that there was no way that he would turn on his friends even if death was staring him in the face.

"I'm glad to see you have a sense of humor considering your situation," Dolla said with a sinister grin.

Smack! Smack!

Dolla smacked Murder across the face twice, causing blood to run from his lip and nose.

"Now, take this you piece of shit!" Dolla grinned, grabbing the bowl of hot honey and pouring over the top of Murder's head.

Murder let a gut-wrenching scream that could have awakened the dead, and then he started to laugh through the pain, knowing that death was around the corner for him.

"Fuck you! I'll see you all in hell!" Murder screamed as he spit blood in the direction of Slick and Dolla.

"I don't think so. You're the only one going to hell, along with your weak ass friends," Cee-Lo interjected as he walked into the basement, carrying a huge container of bees. "Now, who's the bitch, nigga?" Cee-Lo grinned as he raised the container filled with bees over Murder's head, listening to the bees buzzing in anticipation of getting to the honey.

"You're a coward and your punk-ass little crew are cowards!" Murder yelled as he watched Cee-Lo unscrew the jar to and allow the bees to cover his body.

The bees stung him time after time until death consumed his body. Cee-Lo and his crew ran out of the door, slamming it shut behind them. Murder's naked body fell to the ground with over a thousand bees covering it.

"Now, that is one down, but if we catch up to Hannibal before we get the rest of them, I want you to leave him for me," Cee-Lo instructed, cracking a smile at the thought of burying Hannibal alive in a pit of ants.

"With pleasure," Dolla stated, cracking a smile of his own at the thought of watching every member of this crew die slowly and painfully.

SEVEN

At around three o'clock that same afternoon, Lamar angrily paced the floor of one of their hideouts. He was pissed off after receiving the latest news concerning the gruesome killing of his friend, Murder.

"Yo, Lamar, what the fuck is this I hear about them punk ass niggas killin' Murder?" Gunslanger asked as he walked into the house, noticing the rest of the crew sitting around with long faces.

"Yeah, them mutha'fucka's tortured our man by pouring hot honey all over him, and then throwing a gang of bees on him," Lamar replied, feeling completely remorseful yet extremely angry.

"Damn, that's fucked up!" Gunslanger said as he lowered his head, visualizing Murder as he suffered that type of death.

"Yo, we got to strike back, and I mean strike back hard. We need to put this shit to bed fast," Bey spoke up in anger, thinking about catching one of the haters and torturing him the Hustla'z Inc. way.

"You damn right! We need to strike back hard!" OJ chimed in, feeling responsible for his homeboy being killed being that he was the last one of the crew to see him alive.

Murder and OJ were together at a club, but OJ left to go check-in on the block with promises of returning but he never did.

"I'm feeling that shit too!" Gunslanger chimed in with overwhelming enthusiasm. "Do you think we should let Hannibal know about what happened?" Gunslanger asked, directing his question to Lamar.

"Hannibal isn't here right now and I am. I'm going to take the lead on this one, and were going to bury these niggas one at a time. You feel me?" Lamar stated, committed to seeking revenge on everyone involved in the murder of one of their own. "Yo, Gunslanger, I want you to see what that nosey bitch Rasheeda might being hearing on the street."

"Everything is already in motion. I have all my people with their eyes and ears open. I told them to call me immediately with any kind of news, day or night. I'm hearing one of the niggas be kickin' it with that hoodrat bitch, Shelley. The only problem is that I don't know where and I don't have a name yet, but it won't be long before the snake shows its head," Gunslanger stated confidently, remembering having mutted Shelley out after taking her home one night after the club.

"Word! Please say you know where she lives at?" Lamar inquired, staring at Gunslanger with anticipation that he was going to say yes.

"Man, you know I'm already on it. I told one of my little dudes to track her ass down and follow her until she hooks up with a nigga. The first nigga she gets spotted with gets it," Gunslanger stated.

"Find out where she lives, and then pull that little nigga off her. This shit is too important for one of your little niggas to handle. We need to do this ourselves. Once he finds out where she lives we're going to take turns watchin' this bitch until she leads us to who were looking for. It's an out of town dude so make sure it's not somebody we know. Let's try to get this right the first time out. I want to take the dude alive and find out what he knows. Y'all feel me?" Lamar asked as he looked around at everyone for confirmation.

"We feel ya," Bey stated, speaking for everyone.

"Now, who wants to take first post?" Lamar asked, watching everyone's body language for any sign of hesitation.

"I'm down," Lord Jamar stated, speaking for the first time.

"Count me in too," Gunslanger stated as he jumped up from his seat.

"Cool! Now, let's show these fools that they crossed the wrong mutha'fucka's!" Lamar stated as he stood from his seat. "This is for the homie, Murder!"

The all exited the room with revenge on their minds and hearts.

*****

As Hannibal continued to sail down the highway he allowed his thoughts to drift to all the reoccurring drama in his life, starting with the killing of his two street turf enemies Monk and Marlo, leading up to the death of their relative Twin, and then the death of Keisha.

"Man, this hustle game is becoming more twisted by the minute," Hannibal mumbled under his breath as he held his eyes shut for a split second to avoid shedding a tear.

In his mind, he could visualize Keisha smiling at him and having his back, and then in an instant he could visualize her laid out naked with her brains blown out.

Hannibal shook himself out of his daze, and he picked up his phone so that he could let Burna know that he was in town. He pulled over to the nearest gas station and dialed Burna's cell phone and within ten minutes he was following his escort to Burna's locations. They rode through town for about ten minutes to a gated community. Once they got to the house, Hannibal stepped out of the car and looked around. The house was immaculate and Hannibal had to give it to Burna because he must have been pulling in some major money. Burna stood in the doorway waiting to greet him.

"What's up, fam? I see you still holding it down," Hannibal excitedly acknowledged with a smile as he approached Burna.

"Just doing me, fam. You heard me?" Burna asked, cracking a smile as they shook hands and gave each other a manly hug.

As they stepped inside, Hannibal noticed this bad ass female with long jet-black silky hair, a redbone complexioned goddess sitting on the on the couch in the sitting room. She rose to greet Hannibal but when she did she made a point to spread her legs, exposing nothing but a hairy-ass pussy that smiled in Hannibal's face.

"True, so very true," Hannibal commented with a smile, noticing the young lady making her play.

Hannibal quickly took notice that Burna was still rocking his trademark dew rag and eye patch from a shooting he was involved in several years prior.

"Fam, this is my gangsta boo, Danger," Burna introduced her with a smile as he pointed a finger towards her, and then he pointed a finger towards Hannibal. "Babygirl, this is my man, Hannibal."

"It's a pleasure to meet you, Hannibal," Danger stated as she extended her hand towards him.

"Likewise, but if I may inquire, what's up with a beautiful woman such as yourself having a name like Danger?" Hannibal asked as he took her hand in his and looked her directly in the eyes.

"I'm sure you will find out the answer to that in due time, baby. All things will soon come to the light for you," Danger replied softly as she cracked a warm smile, and she faced Burna and winked her eye at him. "Ain't that right, daddy?"

"Yeah, momma, you on it," Burna replied with a sly grin.

Hannibal couldn't help but to continue to wonder why this girl was called Danger.

After they relaxed for a minute, Burna suggested that they take a little ride because he had a piece of business he needed to go handle on the other side of town. Thirty minutes later, they pulled up on an all-out get money stroll that Burna liked to call, *Get Money Strip*. Everything from pimping hoes to selling drugs went down. What really caught Hannibal's attention is when he saw how Danger effortlessly hid a razor blade in her mouth like a skilled assassin before they left.

"Daddy, there that fool goes right there," Danger spoke up, as she quickly pointed a finger in the direction of a guy standing on the corner ahead of them.

The guy was smoking a blunt while fake mackin' to two white prostitutes and showcasing his pint-sized bankroll.

"I've got my eyes on him, babygirl," Burna responded, locking his eyes on the guy they knew as Ray.

Ray was playing games with Burna's money and not taking him serious when Burna told him that he needed to have his five grand to him immediately or he was going to face the consequences.

"Babygirl, go make daddy happy. Make sure you show my man Hannibal here why they call you Danger," Burna stated as he pulled his black-on-black Ranger Rover over the curb, giving Hannibal a sly grin. "Now, you just sit back and what the show."

"My pleasure, daddy!" Danger stated with a smile as she stepped out of the car and walked towards Ray as if she was just another prostitute working the stroll.

As she walked in Ray's direction the other guys out there couldn't help but to take notice of the sexy woman that passed them by. Ray continued to stand on the corner trying to convince these two blond haired bitches to suck and fuck him for a little bit of nothing.

"Why don't you bitches stop with the bullshit and hook a brotha up!" Ray pleaded as he grabbed the arm of the woman that stood at 6'3" with tan skin and an ass that would make any man take notice.

"We done told you once, but you just not tryin' to understand, we want two hundred dollars apiece. We said we'll suck ya' dick and let you fuck us both," the other Taylor Swift look alike prostitute spoke up, noticing Danger as she strutted in their direction with a cunning smile on her face.

"Bitch, I done told your dumb ass that I'm only paying a C-note for the both of you bitches. What the fuck don't you understand?" Ray responded aggressively, losing his patience with the both of them.

He looked up and noticed Danger as she walked in his direction and the sight of her brought a lustful smile to his face.

"Fuck both you bitches! I see me another bad bitch that will gladly take my money," Ray stated, flipping the script on them and instantly walking off from the women.

Ray was mesmerized by this woman's beauty and he couldn't help but hope that she was a full-fledged freak. "Hey, baby!" Ray called out, waving Danger over to him while holding his crotch in his hand.

"You want this pussy, baby?" Danger asked as she stepped up to Ray and immediately began to rub her hands on his dick through his pants.

"You already know the answer to that," Ray answered hastily as he rubbed his hand all over Danger's ass.

"Well, you need to tell those bitches over there to step off," Danger demanded as she played with his belt buckle as if she was trying to get his dick out of his pants right there on the street.

Ray looked over his shoulder, and then said, "You heard the lady. You bitches need to bust a mutha'fuckin' move now!" Ray yelled, giving the two white prostitutes the meanest mug he could muster.

"Fuck you! You ain't shit anyway with your cheap ass!" the amazon tall prostitute yelled out without hesitation.

"And I hope she gets all your fucking money, and I hope he gives your nasty as the clap!" the Taylor Swift look alike prostitute angrily shouted as she joined her friend to walk down the strip.

"Whatever bitch! That shit will only happen in your dreams! Now carry your tired ass down the street, hoe!" Ray responded with a laugh as he turned his attention back to Danger. "Now let's get down to business here," Ray stated with a lustful smile as he rubbed his hand across his crotch.

"Ok, baby, but first let momma her you say you want this pussy," Danger teased while stroking Ray's dick through his pants.

"Yeah, baby, I want that pussy," Ray responded, feeling totally seduced by Danger.

"Okay, daddy, follow me right over here to the alley and let momma give you some of this good stuff," Danger instructed as she turned to walk away.

As she walked she quickly took the razor out of her mouth and cupped it in her hand.

"I'm right behind you," Ray stated as he started to walk behind Danger.

Once they reached the alley, Danger turned around and tugged at Ray's pants. She pulled at Ray's zipper and released his hard dick from his pants. Ray leaned his head back and closed his eyes in anticipation of Danger's mouth engulfing his dick. Danger positioned herself on her knees in front of Ray and took his dick in her hand.

"Yeah, you trick ass nigga, Burna sends his regards!" Danger yelled out, and then with one swift motion she sliced through his dick.

Ray screamed in pain as blood gushed everywhere. Ray fell to the ground as he continued to bleed out.

Danger took his dick and stuffed it in his mouth, and then said, "Yeah, you trick ass nigga, don't nobody fuck over Burna."

Danger turned and walked out of the alley, leaving Ray bleeding and screaming in pain. She walked back to the car as Burna and Hannibal watched her every move.

"What's done is done," Danger stated as she closed the car door behind her and Burna merged into traffic.

Hannibal burst into laughter at the thought of Ray falling for a pretty face and a phat ass.

"Damn, babygirl is the truth. Now I see why you call her Danger," Hannibal commented.

"Yeah, that's my gangsta bitch right there," Burna stated proudly as he admired Danger through the rearview mirror.

"I hear you, bro," Hannibal acknowledged with a smile. "That's the kind of bitch I need right there."

"Yo, I'm gonna send her wit' you for a minute. She should be able to help you put an end to the bullshit you going through right now," Burna stated as he winked at Danger through the rearview mirror.

"Good looking out, fam. I can definitely use her right now," Hannibal replied as he dapped knuckles with Burna.

"Daddy, are you happy now?" Danger asked as she started to take her bloody clothes off.

Danger was not at all shy about the fact that Hannibal was able to see her naked.

"Yeah, I'm pleased with the work you just put. It needed to be done," Burna stated as he turned around to face Danger. "Now, I have one more task for you."

"Anything you need, daddy," Danger humbly responded with a smile, looking deep into Burna's eyes.

"I need you to roll with my man Hannibal for a minute. I want you to be that bottom bitch for him over the next couple of weeks. You feel me?" Burna asked as he looked over at Hannibal with a smile.

"Okay, daddy. Your wish is my command," Danger responded as she looked at Hannibal with a warm smile. "Hannibal, for the next couple of weeks if there is anything you need all you have to do is say the word and I got you."

"That's what I like to hear," Hannibal commented as he returned her smile. "Good lookin', fam. I owe you one."

"No, you don't. Just make sure you send her back in one piece," Burna stated as he cracked a grin. "Now, let's go and enjoy ourselves for the rest of the day."

EIGHT

Three days later, at around sunset, Bey and OJ sat inside one of their undercover cars smoking on a blunt and listening to Scarface's, *My Mind is Playing Tricks on Me*. They were keeping a watchful eye on Shelley's house, hoping that they would get lucky and catch her creeping for a late-night bootie call. They were determined that they were going to light up the first dude they saw her with.

"Yo, who is that nigga right there?" OJ asked Bey as he sat up in the driver's seat to get a better look at the guy walking up to Shelley's door.

"I don't know but when he comes out he is definitely going to catch a bullet," Bey replied as he cocked a bullet into the chamber of his 9 mm Glock.

"I don't want to wait. Let's go pay homie a visit right now," OJ stated as he cocked a bullet into the chamber of his 9 mm Glock and pulled the ski mask down over his face. "Yo, Bey, let's move now just in case this nigga comes right back out."

"Okay, let's do this," Bey said in agreeance with OJ.

They both eased out of the Chevy Impala and eased up to Shelley's front door.

"Yo, Bey, when she opens that door lets rush her ass. If it moves it dies," OJ chimed in just before he banged on the front door.

"I'm a let them both have it right off the rip."

"No, we need him alive. We need to find out who is behind this shit," OJ stated just above a whisper.

Shelley came to the door and she was greeted by the butt of Bey's gun as he smacked her in the forehead, and then shot her in the chest twice.

"Surprise, nigga! Get your ass up right now!" OJ shouted as he pointed the gun at the guy that was sitting on the couch. "What the fuck is your name?"

The guy was totally caught off guard by the two intruders.

"That's right nigga it's just us," Bey stated as he pointed his gun in the guy's face. "Didn't you hear my man ask you your name, nigga?"

"I'm Dade. I don't know what you niggas are up to, but I don't have shit to do with shit," the guy stated just before Bey hit him in the side of the head with the butt of his gun.

Smack!

Dade's vision became blurry, and he fell to the ground.

"Get your ass up! Your comin' with us," Bey stated as he grabbed the dude by the arm and yanked him off the ground. "Yo, grab his car and follow me," Bey instructed, feeling his adrenaline in overdrive.

"I'm on it," OJ stated as he reached and grabbed the car keys out of Dade's pocket.

He swiftly walked Dade over to his car, popped the trunk, and shoved him inside.

*****

Later that night inside the basement of the hideout in the Brady Heights district, Dade hung from the ceiling by his feet while staring into an aquarium filled with piranhas. He hoped that he would be able to make it out of this ordeal alive.

"Help! Help!" Dade screamed, hearing only his echoes returning his screams as he tried to reach up and free himself from bondage.

"Oh, lookie here! Our man Dade is trying to get free. Nigga you better be still. You get your feet free and your gonna be greeted by our friends down there," OJ stated sarcastically as he walked into the basement with an evil grin on his face followed by the rest of the members of Hustla'z Inc. except for Hannibal.

"Untie me, please! I didn't kill nobody! I don't know what the fuck you niggas are talkin' about!" Dade screamed out, sensing that he was about to be tortured by the guys that surrounded him.

"Well, it looks like somebody is trying to tap out, and we haven't even begun to have fun yet," Lamar remarked with a cunning grin.

"P-P-Please don't kill me! I'll tell y'all what you want to know, but I'm tellin' you that I didn't kill anyone," Dade pleaded, feeling his own urine running down his chest and up to his mouth.

"Man, this nigga is pissing on his self," Gunslanger stated as he burst out in laughter.

He was joined in laughter by everyone else as they watched Dade's urine dripping to the floor.

"Damn, homie, you can't hold your bladder can you," Lamar taunted in laughter as he pushed the button that controlled the rope, causing it to lower Dade five more inches closer to the aquarium.

The piranhas began to jump from the water at the scent of Dade's human flesh.

"No, please don't kill me! I swear I don't know who is behind this! I'm just a worker! I don't call the shots!" Dade screamed out, noticing that he was being lowered closer-and-closer to the man-eating fish.

"Okay, Dade. So, you tellin' me that you just a slave. I get it, but now you need to tell me whose you're master. I'm gonna give you one chance to win your freedom and one chance only, and if you don't say what I want to hear your going swimming. You agree?" Lamar deceivingly proposed with a straight face.

"Yeah, man, I agree! I'll tell you everything I know," Dade replied fearfully as a one of the fish came inches from biting his nose off.

"First, I'm going to ask you several questions and if you answer honestly I will raise you up, but if I think your lying I'm going to lower your ass down some more. Your fate is in your hands, Dade."

"Okay! Okay!" Dade shouted in agreement as his body was lowered one more inch and one of the piranhas bit a chunk out of his cheek.

"Oops, my bad. Sorry 'bout that," Lamar said with a laugh as he hit the switch and raised Dade out of the range of the fish. "Now, Dade, I want to know who ordered the hit on Murder?" Lamar asked as he waved the switch in Dade's face.

"Man, it was Cee-Lo!" Dade hastily stated, thinking about only one thing and that was trying to save his life.

"Fam, do you think this nigga is tellin' the truth?" Lamar asked, turning around to face his friends.

"Man, I don't know," Gunslanger stated with a laugh.

"Man, that nigga ain't lying! Stall the fool out, Lamar," OJ said as he lit his Newport and took a long pull off of it.

Lamar looked back over to Dade and he could see a single tear falling down his cheek. Lamar wasn't getting much joy out of the task at hand, but with Hannibal out of reach he felt he had to do what he had to do. The leadership of the group was left up to him since Hannibal wasn't around. He just hoped that the information he was gathering would prove beneficial.

"Alright, Mr. Sensitive. Dade, I guess God is on your side today," Lamar said, turning back around to face Dade.

"Hey, man, I told you everything I know!" Dade screamed as he urinated on himself again due to the fear of not being alive anymore.

"Now, Dade, I want to know who this Cee-Lo guy works for? Who is he taking orders from? I know you work for Cee-Lo, but I want to know who the head nigga is. I need him," Lamar stated as he waved the switch in front of Dade's face again.

"Man, they come from Florida! I didn't have anything to do with none of this shit! I just work for Cee-Lo on some side shit. It was Slick, Dolla, and Cee-Lo that killed Murder! I didn't have shit to do with shit! I'm tellin' you the truth!" Dade stated in the most convincing voice that he could muster.

"Oh yeah!" Lamar remarked with a frown at the words of his man Murder being killed by some unknown haters. "Y'all believe this nigga?"

"Yeah, I believe the nigga for now, but we need to check this nigga's info out. We don't even know these dudes. This shit is gonna be like lookin' for a needle in a haystack," Gunslanger remarked as everyone shook their head in agreeance.

"Dade! Dade! Dade! You sound convincing to them but not to me. I'm gonna give you one more time to clear your name from this shit and live," Lamar expressed, shaking his head from side-to-side as he pushed the button to lower Dade down ten inches.

A piranha leaped up and latched on to Dade's nose with its razor-sharp teeth, biting it off his face. Dade screamed out in agony as blood gushed out. Lamar raised him back up because he did not want him dead just yet. He had a little more information that he needed to squeeze out of Dade before he met his final fate.

"Now, Dade, I want you to tell me where I can find Cee-Lo and the rest of those punk ass niggas!" Lamar said with a smile as he hit the switch and lowered Dade five inches, causing him to cry out in fear. "Opps, my bad!"

"They set-up house in this pink house off of forty-sixth street. I've never been there but that's where you can find him," Dade stated as another tear rolled down his cheek. "Lord, please don't let me die!"

"So, what do y'all think? Has this nigga done enough to deserve his life or do we feed him to the fishes?" Lamar asked, turning around to face his crew, noticing impatience on their faces.

"Man, let the punk ass nigga go. He can serve another purpose," Lord Jamar stated as he walked towards the door of the basement.

"Well Dade, I guess you have convinced my people that you deserve to live but my man Murder thinks different. So, I want you to give him a message from his homies when you go to hell. I want you to tell him it's gonna be a lot of company with him soon," Lamar stated with a grin before hitting the switch and watching Dade being lowered into the aquarium.

"No!" Dade screamed before his head hit the water, causing a swarm of piranhas to rush him.

Dade's body flipped over several times before it laid still as the piranhas devoured him.

Moments later, Lamar, Gunslanger, Bey, and the rest of the crew stood in pleasure as they watched the remainder of Dade's flesh being eaten away, leaving only bones in the water to float to the top.

"Now, I want you all to understand that this is only the beginning, and if Dade was telling the truth we now have the heads up on some of the niggas that are behind this bullshit. We need to find them and get to the head of this mess. So, let's gear up and go pay these niggas a little visit. I want to take the nigga named Cee-Lo alive. I want to leave him for Hannibal," Lamar stated as he grabbed his 9 mm and stuck it into his waistband.

"We feel you," Gunslanger acknowledged with a sinister grin and a head nod.

"What do you want us to do with all of this shit?" Bey asked as he pointed towards the aquarium.

"What do you think I want you to do? Take that aquarium and drop it off in the Arkansas river. It's not enough of the nigga left to be a problem so we good on that. You feel me?" Lamar said before he cracked a grin and took a long pull off the blunt he had in his hand. "Who are we?"

"Hustla'z Inc.!" the all shouted in unison as they all turned to leave, having only thoughts of revenge on their minds.

NINE

Lamar and the rest of Hustla'z Inc. exited the house with one purpose in mind and that was to go scope out the house that Dade stated the guys behind the death of Murder would be at. As Lamar got into his GMC Yukon, he picked up his cell phone to call Hannibal and give him the heads up on the progress that he had made in finding out who was coming at them. It had been a couple days since they had spoken to each other and he thought that was really weird.

"What's up?" Hannibal asked when he answered the phone on the third ring.

"Man, just takin' care of business. I called to tell you that they hit Murder the other day. They took him out on some torture type shit, but I don't think he talked. We made some progress in finding out who is behind all this bullshit. We grabbed this little punk ass nigga and strung his ass up. He lasted ten minutes, and then he started singing like a little canary. He said that we can find some of the guys at a house off of forty-sixth street. We about to head over there now to see what the scene looks like. Anyway, where the fuck you been? You been out of pocket for a minute now."

"Man, I was at my duck off down in Houston. I just needed to get away for a bit, but that shit got all fucked up. Some people tried to break in on me, but I saw them before they could get in and popped off a few rounds at 'em. I don't know if I hit them but they got away before I could get a good look at 'em. I think all this shit is connected somehow, but I just haven't been able to put my finger on it."

"We were told that it's a dude named Cee-Lo that's behind everything up this way. I'ma leave him for you once we get him, but everyone else up here is dead meat. When you heading back this way?" Lamar inquired.

"I'm on my way there now. I had to make a stop in Baton Rouge first. I'm bringing back someone that may be able to help us to settle this shit for good. I want to put this shit to rest. I'm sick and tired of this shit. Go scope the house out that you we're talking about, but don't make a move on them until I get there. I should there and rested up by morning. I'll hit you up when I get there. We need to have a talk," Hannibal stated as he sped down the highway towards Tulsa. "Hey, before I go, I want you to see if you can find that nigga Dee. Tell him I need to talk to him and his man A.S.A.P. He will know who and why."

"I got you. Consider it done," Lamar stated with confidence.

"I'm gone," Hannibal stated before he ended the call.

Hannibal looked over at Danger who was asleep in the passenger's seat. He could not believe someone so beautiful was also so deadly. If she proved to be as big an asset to him as she was to Burna, Hannibal planned to make her an offer she could not refuse. He needed another down ass bitch since Keisha was out of the picture.

*****

Within an hour, Lamar, Bey, and OJ sat down the street from the pink house located on Iroquois off of 46th Street. It was not hard to find given the color. They watched as people came and left for about two hours. It wasn't hard to tell which one of the guys was Cee-Lo. They could tell because he was the one giving orders and talking on his cell phone.

They observed that there were only three guys with Cee-Lo but they never traveled alone. If one person left they all would leave. The would make confronting them a little complicated but not impossible. They came up with a plan to hit them at night once they figured that they would not be leaving again. They would make it quick to try and minimize the chance of one of them getting hit in the process.

Hannibal arrived back to Tulsa at around eleven o'clock that evening. He decided that they would just check into a hotel because he didn't want to take Danger to his sister's apartment because it was so late. They checked into the *Doubletree Hotel* in the downtown area. Once he got settled in, he decided to give Lamar a call to let him know he was in town and to also get the heads up on what Lamar knew about this Cee-Lo character.

"Hello," Lamar answered in a groggy tone of voice.

"Yo, it's me. Sorry to wake you up, but I wanted to let you know that I made it into town. I'm at the Doubletree downtown. What did you find out?"

"We found the house. Them fools are some sittin' ducks. We figured we would hit them at night once they are in for the night because they travel in packs. When one leaves they all leave," Lamar stated.

"Man, we need to have a talk 'cause I thought I told you we weren't doin' this shoot 'em up bang bang shit anymore," Hannibal stated with a bit of irritation in his voice.

"Well, you haven't been around, and once Murder got hit what did you expect me to do?" Lamar asked.

"I expected you to use your fuckin' head. You could have used restraint but instead you've gone and started an all-out war. We could have used the people that work for us to get to the bottom of this shit and kept ourselves out of the equation. Now if we don't get involved we'll look weak, but your right I haven't been here so I guess you did what you thought was right. I'm not gonna keep beatin' a dead horse. I'ma gonna hit you up in the morning. Get everybody together so we can go over the plan. I don't want anybody to get hit if we can help it. Did you locate Dee?" Hannibal asked.

"Yeah, I got with him. I told him you want to see him and his man and that I would call him once you got here. I'll set somethin' up with him for tomorrow afternoon. Now, I'ma take my black ass back to sleep. It's been a long day," Lamar said as he let out a long yawn.

"Alright, sleepy head. Get with me in the mornin'," Hannibal stated before he hit the end button.

Hannibal went into the bedroom of the suite he was staying in and decided to also go to sleep. He knew tomorrow would be a very long day for him.

*****

"Who is this callin' me at six in the mornin', the crack of dawnin," Lamar sang along with his favorite song by Notorious B.I.G. as he bent a couple of corners that morning to re-up the drugs at one of the stash spots.

Once he was done, he decided to return home and wait for Hannibal to give him a call so that they could meet up. Lamar whipped his Mercedes-Benz into the parking space next to his GMC Yukon then he noticed a Ford F-150 with furniture strapped on to it parked four spaces down.

"There goes the neighborhood!" Lamar stated to himself as he exited his car.

Then with a sense of urgency he bent down and reached under the driver's seat to grab the black duffel bag filled with the weeks take from the stash house he had just left.

Knock! Knock!

Guru was dressed up as a little girl. He was wearing a wig and a pink summer dress. He lightly tapped on Lamar's driver's side window with one hand with his other hand behind his back gripping a 9 mm Glock.

"Yeah!" Lamar stated, being startled by the tapping on the window.

He quickly raised his head out of the car, leaving the duffel bag sitting on the driver's seat.

"What's up young lady?" Lamar asked as he forced a smile.

"This is what's up!" Guru replied just before he pulled the gun from behind his back and shot Lamar twice in the chest.

Blak! Blak!

Lamar was totally caught off guard and never saw what was coming. He stumbled backwards, and then took two steps forwards before for he fell face first.

"Here's to fuckin' wit' the wrong people!" Guru shouted with a grin as he walked over to Lamar and put two more shots into his back.

Blak! Blak!

Guru walked off then gave his brother Ace the heads up that he had finished Lamar off.

"Bro, that nigga is history," Guru confirmed with a smile after he jumped into the Ford F-150, removing the fake wig from his head.

"Good! Very good! Now, let's go chill and wait for this other fool to pop up on the scene so we can end this madness. I want to get the fuck out of town before the shit hits the fan. You feel me?" Ace asked.

"Yep! This ain't nothin' but a day's work," Guru stated as he dapped knuckles with his older brother and grabbed the half smoked blunt out of the ashtray and lit it up.

He took several long pulls on it and then exhaled a cloud of smoke through his nose, feeling the craftiness of his work.

"You got that right, lil' bro," Ace commented with a smile as he put the truck in reverse and backed out of the parking space.

Hannibal had been calling Lamar's cell phone for ten minutes and he didn't get an answer. He decided to pop by Lamar's condo to see what the hold-up was. He was growing impatient and wanted to get down to business. As he pulled into the parking garage, he noticed that the driver's side door to his cousin's Mercedes-Benz was wide open, causing an uncomfortable feeling. He sensed something wasn't right because his cousin loved that car, and he would never leave the door open like that. He quickly put his truck in park and grabbed his .40 caliber Desert Eagle out of his shoulder holster. Hannibal rushed over to his cousin's car, and was shocked by what he saw.

"No! No! Please say it ain't so!" Hannibal screamed as he rushed over to his cousin's aide, noticing that Lamar had been shot and left for dead.

He hurried and grabbed his cousin off of the ground and placed him in the backseat of his truck.

"Hold on, cuz!" Hannibal mumbled under his breath as he sped out of the parking garage and down Denver Avenue.

It was a good thing that they were only a couple minutes away from *OSU Medical Center*. Hannibal nearly crashed into an ambulance as he sped into the emergency area of the hospital.

"Shit!" Hannibal shouted as he slammed the truck into park and rushed to get Lamar out of the backseat and into the hospital. "Get me some fuckin' help!"

His shouting quickly caught the attention of the medical staff and they rushed to his aide with a stretcher. They rushed Lamar into the back, then down the hall into one of the operating rooms. Hannibal was left standing in the hallway in complete shock.

"Please don't die, cuz! I need you," Hannibal stated before he fell to his knees.

He was covered in blood and sweating profusely. A nurse came and lifted him up by his shoulders and escorted him to the waiting room.

Later that day, Hannibal paced the floor of the hideout they kept on the eastside, while damning himself over-and-over again for not being there to protect his cousin. His mind drifted back to the frightening sight of his cousin lying in the parking garage in a pool of his own blood. Lamar was now laid up in the hospital's intensive care unit with all types of tubes and monitors hooked up to him as he battled for his life.

"Yo, Hannibal, what's the status on Lamar?" Bey asked sympathetically, noticing Hannibal caught up in a hurtful mood.

"As for now he's in a coma. He's fighting for his life. One of the bullets punctured one of his lungs so they have him hooked up to a special breathing machine," Hannibal replied, dropping his head in hurt.

He had a strong urge to strike back at the people responsible, but he did not want to put anyone else in anymore danger.

"Man, that's fucked up!" Gunslanger commented with twisted anger and pain, feeling the same revengeful vibe of everyone in the room. "Yo, we need to go and deal with these niggas head up. Fuck this waiting bullshit. We need to finish what we started before we all be laid up in the hospital."

"I'm feelin' that shit! It's time to get at that nigga Cee-Lo and crush these niggas. You feel me?" Bey asked in an anger tone of voice.

"Fo'sho! We need to get to the bottom of this shit," OJ chimed in.

"Danger, is everything in motion on that nigga Cee-Lo?" Hannibal asked, raising up his head and turning his attention to her.

"Yeah, baby. You just say the word and it's done 'cause that nigga is all up in my shit," Danger replied convincingly, feeling the same revengeful vibe flowing through the room.

Danger was willing to crush Cee-Lo without a second thought.

"I need you to find out who that nigga is working for. I want to eliminate each and everyone one of them. This shit has got to end," Hannibal stated, slightly raising his voice.

"Consider it done. That dumbass nigga will meet me anywhere and anytime. All I have to do is ask," Danger replied.

"Perfect!" Hannibal replied as he forced a smile across his face. "Ok, Danger, here is what I want you to do. I want you to give the fool a call and set up a date with him for tomorrow night. I want you to make sure to end the date at the Doubletree. I already have two suites under a fake name. OJ, Bey, and me will be in the suite next door to you just in case you need some assistance, but I doubt that," Hannibal continued, having every confidence in Danger's capabilities. "Remember, don't kill him until I get to talk to him. Just wound the nigga so that we won't have any trouble out of him. You will be in the suite at the end of the hall so we shouldn't have to worry about the noise too much, but let's not let this shit get too out of hand or we'll all in up in jail."

"Don't worry, Hannibal. I've got everything under control," Danger forewarned with a devilish grin.

"Trust me, boo. I believe you," Hannibal acknowledged with a smile and wink of his eye, remembering Danger's handy work with a razor when she was called upon by Burna. "Now, here is the next move we're going to make. Yo, Gunslanger and Lord Jamar, at about ten o'clock tomorrow night I want y'all to tool up and go hit that house. I want them niggas off balance while she is puttin' in her work. I want them niggas to understand that this all-out war with us from this day forward. You feel me?"

"I feel you, bruh," Gunslanger stated, nodding his head in agreeance.

"Okay, and in the meantime, I'm gonna be arranging for us to get out of town for a while once these bodies start turning up. I don't want us to be around once the heat gets turned up. I've got a meeting with Dee tomorrow. Once Cee-Lo is dropped and we have the identity of who he works for I'm gonna give that job to him and his people. I think we need a pro for that one," Hannibal stated as he cracked a huge smile, feeling a little better about the whole situation.

He stood up and walked to a closet down the hallway. He reached in and grabbed a huge Louis Vuitton suitcase. He opened one of the suitcases and removed five manila envelopes from it and placed them on the table. Each envelope had one of their names written on it.

"Inside of these envelopes are your vacation packages, consisting of a fifty-thousand-dollar cashier's check, a call in advance plane ticket, and a burner phone preprogrammed with each of our phone numbers. You can go anywhere you would like to go in the world. We will meet back here in three months. Hopefully by that time we will have Lamar back with us, and all of this bullshit will be a thing of the past. So, until we meet again, let's swiftly crush our enemies and enjoy ourselves in peace." Hannibal said with a smile even though he wanted to frown.

"To our homie, Lamar!" Wild Bill spoke up.

"To Hustla'z Inc," Bey chimed in.

"To Hustla'z Inc," everyone shouted as they all raised their glasses into the air.

They were committed to seeking revenge with an iron fist in order to avenge the shooting of Lamar and the killing of Murder.

*****

A block away, sitting in an unmarked van equipped with high tech listening devices and computers, Detective Jenkins and his partner Detective Finley listened attentively to Hannibal and his crew as they formulated their plan to seek revenge on those that shot Lamar and killed Murder.

"Hey, Jenkins, did you hear what I just heard? These boys are planning to commit at least two murders, and then skip town," Detective Finley asked as he typed some information into one of the computers mounted in front of him.

He wanted to make sure that all the information that they received was documented properly.

"Yeah, I heard those idiots. They think they have the game all figured out," Detective Jenkins replied, putting back on his headset before he pushed the rewind button so that he could listen to the whole conversation again.

"This shit works like a fuckin' charm," Detective Finley stated with a smile.

"Yep, we need to thank them good ole boys over there at the FBI for this shit," Detective Jenkins chipped in, sharing the same satisfying smile.

"So, detective, what do you know about this new girl that they call Danger. I haven't seen or heard of her before. She must not be from around here. Hannibal is breaking out all the big guns for this one," Detective Finley remarked.

"Yeah, I would say her job is to take out Cee-Lo once she's gotten some information from him. I'm thinking that if she can't get him to talk they plan on torturing him for the info," Detective Jenkins analyzed while still allowing his mind to play through several other scenarios that could take place once they had Cee-Lo at the Doubletree Hotel.

"That sounds about right to me. I want to hear that part where he is tellin' this Danger what to do again,"

Detective Finley stating, thinking that they may have missed something.

"I think we pretty much got it all, but sure I'll play it again," Detective Jenkins said as he hit the play button on the recorder.

"Nah, I think Hannibal has something else going on that he didn't tell them about. Plus, I think we need to try and learn a little more about this female. She might be able to lead us to an even bigger fish than Hannibal. We already got him on conspiracy to commit murder with tonight's recording alone. If we pick her up and squeeze her just right, we might get her to flip. These gangsta bitches talk a good game but once that jail time starts to sink in they act different," Detective Finley concluded.

"I think you might be on to somethin'. We need to get a photograph of her and run her through the facial recognition database. We might get a hit, and find out who she really is that way. If her momma put down the crack pipe or the bottle for a little while I know her real name can't be Danger," Detective Jenkins remarked with a laugh.

"Detective, the more I think about it the more it makes sense to me, being that the last person Cee-Lo would suspect of killing him would be the very woman in his bed," Detective Finley concluded.

"That sounds logical to me, detective," Detective Jenkins stated with a smile as he continued to log the information into the computer database, confirming Danger and Cee-Lo's involvement in this gang war. "Well, I guess we can conclude our surveillance analysis for the evening. I think we have everything we need to diffuse an all-out gang war. We can start typing for warrants and round these jokers up once and for all. Wouldn't you agree?"

"I sure do. This could be a career case if we're able to bring down Hannibal and his band of thieves. Plus, I have wanted this Cee-Lo for a while. I have always suspected him of killing Detective Rogers but I couldn't never prove it," Detective Finley stated as he crisscrossed his arms over his chest.

TEN

The following night at around eight o'clock, Hannibal sat beside Lamar's bed in the intensive care unit fighting back his tears at the sight of his cousin hooked up to all the sophisticated medical equipment. He was fighting for his life with every bit of strength in his body.

"Cuz, stay strong. Fight that death 'cause I need you here with me," Hannibal stated softly as he held Lamar's hand, placing his head on the bed to say a quick prayer. "So, until we meet on solid ground I want you to know that I love you with all my heart. I never meant for this to happen, but it will not end with you."

Hannibal leaned over and kissed Lamar on the forehead, and then walked out of the intensive care unit. Hannibal was determined to punish every person on the face of the earth that had anything to do with the shooting of his favorite cousin.

Across town Cee-Lo's cell phone vibrated at approximately eight-thirty p.m., forcing him to stop his conversation with the guys that had come up to Tulsa with him. He saw Danger's cell phone number showing on the display.

"What's good, ma?" Cee-Lo asked with excitement, answering his phone on the second ring.

He stepped away from the group of guys as they continued to talk and laugh while passing blunt after blunt around the table.

"What do you think I want? I'm trying to hook up with you tonight," Danger replied seductively, sounding just as excited as Cee-Lo.

"Is that right? I guess we can try and make that happen," Cee-Lo responded hesitantly, giving off the impression that hooking up with her for the night was not such a big deal.

A lustful smile came across his face at the thought of working Danger's sexy body all night long.

"You better make it happen after everything I've gone through to look this good for you tonight," Danger responded deceivingly, playing along with Cee-Lo and his little game.

Danger forced herself to sound as if she was catching a little bit of an attitude since he was acting as if he was considering not going out on a date with her.

"Damn, shorty, calm the fuck down! I don't have time for the bullshit," Cee-Lo said with a giggle.

Cee-Lo was convinced that after he hooked up with Danger tonight and he hit her with some good dick that she would be on lock with him for good.

"Shorty, give me about an hour to go to the crib, take a shower, change my clothes, and then I'm all yours for the evening," Cee-Lo stated as he winked his eye at one of his homies that was looking in his direction.

"Ok, Mr. Smooth, I'll be waiting, but you better not have me waiting too long 'cause I'm already starving," Danger stated as a sinister grin came across her face at the thought of slitting Cee-Lo's throat from ear-to-ear.

Danger had anticipated having to work harder to kill a nigga like Cee-Lo, but he was such a fool for a big ass and a smile that he made it easy.

"I gotcha, shorty. I'll hit you when I'm on my way," Cee-Lo stated before he ended the call.

His homie Trey walked up and passed him one of the blunts that was circulating through the room. He took a long pull on it before passing it right back to Trey.

"Trey, I'm 'bout to get out of here and go holla at this broad. I need you to hold things down 'cause I don't want to be disturbed for the rest of the evening. You feel me?" Cee-Lo said with a big grin on his face.

"Damn, nigga, that bitch got you twisted and I bet you haven't even it hit it yet," Trey commented as he noticed that his friend was spaced out in happiness.

"Anyway, mutha'fucka!" Cee-Lo said as he waved Trey's comment off.

"You know I'm right. Don't worry 'bout nothin' everything is good around here 'cause we got enough heat to start World War III," Trey said as he dapped knuckles with Cee-Lo.

"Alright, man, I'm out," Cee-Lo stated as he swiped his keys off the table and strolled out the front door.

He took a quick look around the neighborhood then quickly walked to his black-on-black Escalade with only the thought of fucking Danger until morning on his mind. Cee-Lo was so distracted with his lustful thoughts that he failed to notice the four cars with blacked out windows parked just as you go to turn the corner off the block.

Gunslanger grabbed his cell phone and called Bey in the follow car behind him.

"Did you see who just passed us?" Gunslanger asked, knowing that it was time to put in work on the niggas that were left at the house up the block.

"Yeah, I saw that little bitch," Bey replied, checking his Rolex watch to confirm that they were still on schedule.

"Well, let's do this for the homies, Lamar and Murder," Gunslanger stated before he ended the call.

Gunslanger then called the guys in the third and fourth cars and told them that they were ready to move and to stay on point. They also had enough firepower to start a war. They were strapped with AK-47's, Tech-Nine's, and 12-gauge shotguns. Normally, they would have done a drive-by and peppered the house up real good, but this was personal so they decided on a different approach.

Click! Click!

They cocked their guns as they stopped two houses down from the house that Cee-Lo's men where held up in. They all hopped out quickly and took their positions surrounding the house. They had the front and the backdoor covered along with each side of the house just in case someone tried to jump out of a window. They didn't want anyone walking away from this hit alive.

"What's up now!" Gunslanger yelled as he kicked the front door of the house in and began to unload the AK-47 he held in his hand.

Blak! Blak! Blak! Blak!

The guys in the house were totally taken off guard. Some tried to hurry and grab their weapons and some tried to run for the backdoor. Those that ran for the backdoor in the small house were met with the sound of a 12-gauge shotgun as Bey let off shot after shot into anyone that moved. The chaos of the mass killings rang out in the night air.

Once Bey had emptied out the shotgun, Lord Jamar rushed into the house and took up a position and let bullets from the Tech-Nine ring out.

"Stop firing! Stop firing!" Gunslanger yelled.

Once the bullets had stopped, the could see the death and devastation that they had caused. Six members of Cee-Lo's crew laid out on the floor of the living room and kitchen in pools of their own blood. Lord Jamar went over and gave each man a final shot to the head to ensure that they are dead. They then quickly made their way back to their cars and sped off down the street. The night was far from over. Now it was time to make sure that Cee-Lo was put to rest in the most gruesome way possible.

*****

Just about a block away, Detective Hightower and Detective Livingston sat in their unmarked police vehicle as they listened to the havoc that was ringing out in this all black neighborhood. They thought about calling the shooting in, but they decided to let it happen since it was just a group of black thugs killing each other. They saw it is a cheap and quick way to eliminate some of the trash that was polluting the streets of Tulsa.

"Fuck 'em. I don't care who dies in that house tonight. No one knows that we're here and let's keep it that way. I want the mutha'fucka's these niggas are working for. I need a big bust, not some small-time playa's that ain't gonna talk," Detective Hightower stated as he listened to the call go out over the radio.

"You know me, I really don't give a fuck. That's just a little less work we'll have to do when we finally take these fools down," Detective Livingston commented as he ran his hands through his hair and looked at himself in the rearview mirror.

"I hear you. Let's wait fifteen minutes, and then head over to the Doubletree. If those niggas make a move there we will take them down," Detective Hightower remarked as he waved his finger in the air.

After waiting fifteen minutes, they took the back way out of the neighborhood and made their way towards the Doubletree Hotel in hopes of making the biggest bust of their careers.

*****

Cuddling in the downtown district at *Lefty's on Greenwood*, Danger and Cee-Lo sat embraced in each other's arms, checking out Charlie Redd and the Full Flava King's as they did their thing on stage.

"Babydoll, this nigga is pretty good," Cee-Lo whispered in Danger's ear.

"Yeah, he has a little star quality about him," Danger commented, trying to give the hint that she was a little bored and wanted to be alone with Cee-Lo.

"Yeah, I get what you're saying. Let's wait until he finishes this set, and then we will get the hell out of here."

Cee-Lo allowed his mind to drift towards romantic events as he rubbed his hand up and down Danger's thigh, often easing his hand all the way up her thigh and brushing against her pussy, sending a flow of sexual desire to his dick.

"You sure you're ready to go?" Danger asked seductively, while flirting with her eyes, which said she was ready to go and be more romantic with the man that sat beside her.

"Yeah, shorty, I'm ready to get the fuck out of here. The drinks are watered down and I can't smoke in this bitch. We should have gone to the ghetto spot and got fucked up. I'm not for all this stuck-up bullshit," Cee-Lo replied, convinced that he was ready to hit the sheets in order to bond their relationship forever.

They walked out the club a little bit after midnight, and headed towards Cee-Lo's truck.

"So, beautiful, where to now?" Cee-Lo whispered into Danger's ear as he embraced her from behind, while grinding his hard dick up against her soft, phat ass.

"Umm, what would you say about going back to my hotel? I know it might be a little uncomfortable, being that we are just getting to know one another," Danger deceivingly remarked, giving Cee-Lo the impression that she was a good girl, while she kept grinding her ass up against his hard dick.

"It won't be a problem as long as we both control ourselves," Cee-Lo replied convincingly, using the common line women used when they were trying not to give it up.

He spun Danger around to face him, and then he passionately kissed her as he grabbed both of her ass cheeks in his hands.

"Damn, you kissing me like we might get me into some trouble tonight," Danger responded teasingly with a blushing smile.

She tongue kissed Cee-Lo deeply as she rubbed her hand up and down his hard dick, giving him the hint that she was feeling him sexually just as much as he was feeling her.

"Well, I know exactly what we need to do," Cee-Lo said with smile as he opened the passenger's side door for Danger, allowing her to slide into the car with her legs wide open as she exposed her hairy pussy to him.

"And may I ask where we goin' now, Mr. Know-It-All?" Danger asked with a curious smile, catching Cee-Lo staring between her legs with a horny smile on his face.

"Where the fuck you think we're goin'? We are heading over to your hotel room," Cee-Lo stated bluntly as he closed the car door and walked around to the driver's side with a lustful smile on his face.

Once Cee-Lo got inside the car Danger said, "Oh, is that so," Danger remarked with a faking smile. "Well, this is your game and I'm just a willing pawn in it. My hotel suite is at the Doubletree off of Denver. I'm in suite seven-thirteen."

"Don't you trip, shorty. I'm gonna let you have plenty of control as soon as we get to the hotel," Cee-Lo stated playfully as he rubbed his hands over Danger's beautiful face, causing her to start to laugh as she brushed his hand away.

Cee-Lo only cracked a lustful smile at her gesture, and then he stuck his hand deep under her mini-skirt and began to finger fuck her. Once his fingers were dripping wet, he removed his fingers from under her skirt and stuck them in his mouth.

"Umm, that shit is tasty," Cee-Lo commented.

"Boy, you so nasty!" Danger commented with laughter, while watching Cee-Lo continue to suck her juices off his fingers like he was sucking on a candy stick.

"I'm only nasty for you, shorty. Just for you," Cee-Lo stated as he turned the ignition and backed out into the street, heading west down Archer towards Denver.

As Cee-Lo made the short drive towards the hotel, he visualized himself fucking and sucking Danger until the sun came up the next morning. Danger sat in the passenger's seat visualizing herself with a blood-soaked blade in her hand as she watched Cee-Lo choke to death on his own blood.

Cee-Lo pulled his truck into the valet parking area five minutes later, he eagerly jumped out of the truck and rushed to open the passenger's door for Danger. Cee-Lo wrapped his arm around Danger's waist and led her into the hotel. They got on the elevator and they both remained silent. There was no need for words. They both knew exactly what was on their minds. Cee-Lo's mind was on sex, while Danger's mind was on nothing but death and destruction. Cee-Lo rubbed his hands all over Danger's body as she continued to massage his dick with such force that he almost came right there in the elevator.

Once they reached Danger's hotel suite, Cee-Lo wrapped his hands around her waist and damn near forced her into the suite while kissing Danger all over her neck.

"Damn, baby, you taste so sweet," Cee-Lo whispered in her ear as he continued to kiss on her.

They walked into the dark room and crashed onto the bed. Cee-Lo pulled Danger on top of him. He stuck his tongue into Danger's mouth and he began to rub his hand over her mini-skirt to find the zipper so that he could remove it. Once he found the zipper, he removed her mini-skirt as she took the blouse off herself. Even though it was dark, Cee-Lo was still marveled by what he saw in front of him.

"Baby, get undressed while I go in the bathroom and freshen up," Danger stated as she sat upright on top of Cee-Lo, looking into his gleaming, lustful eyes.

Danger got up and started to walk towards the bathroom.

"Anything for you, baby. You just make sure you don't take too long in that bathroom," Cee-Lo responded as he obediently began to remove his clothes and shoes.

Once he was done, he laid back on the bed. He was completely naked with his dick sticking straight up in the air.

"Girl, I'm gonna spank the shit out of that ass!" Cee-Lo said with enthusiasm as he looked up at the dark ceiling.

"You better spank this ass good 'cause if you don't this will be the last time you see it," Danger spoke from inside the bathroom as a smile came across her face.

Danger stepped into the bathroom doorway completely naked with both her hands on her hips, allowing the only light in the whole suite that was coming from the bathroom to show off her gorgeous body.

"Damn, girl, you look good!" Cee-Lo shouted as he admired Danger's beauty. "Umm! Um! Um! Um! Girl, bring yo' fine ass over here so I can make this a hell of a night to remember," Cee-Lo stated before he licked his lips.

"You promise this is gonna be a night to remember?" Danger asked as she slowly walked over to the bed.

Danger grabbed Cee-Lo's dick and slowly stroked it up and down.

"I need you to close your eyes for me first. I have somethin' special for you," Danger told him as she looked at him with a smile on her face.

"Whatever you say, baby," Cee-Lo said as he closed his eyes and leaned his head back, anticipating that he was about to get his dick sucked by this beautiful woman.

Danger removed her signature razor from her mouth and raised it high in the air before she stated, "I bring greetings from Hannibal and his crew!"

Within a blink of an eye, she swiped the razor across Cee-Lo's face twice, causing blood to splatter everywhere. Cee-Lo's hands immediately reached for his face, but Danger just kept swing the blade back and forth.

"No!" Cee-Lo screamed as blood poured from his face and arms.

Danger's attacked had managed to remove Cee-Lo's nose from his face, both of his eyes were sliced so that he was unable to see, and the bone in both of his arms could also be seen. Danger stopped and stood back to assess what she might due next to her somewhat helpless enemy. Just as she did so the door to the connecting suite swung open and Hannibal and the rest of Hustla'z Inc. entered the room.

"I want to ask this mutha'fucka some questions before we end his worthless life," Hannibal stated as he motioned for Danger to stop just before she finished the job.

Cee-Lo lay helpless in a pool of his own blood as he shook from the pain that his wounds caused him.

"Who the fuck is there?" Cee-Lo yelled out as he waved his head back and forth but was unable to see his assailants. "Do you know who you fuckin' wit'? Every one of you mutha'fucka's are dead!"

"Yeah, I know exactly who I'm fuckin' wit', nigga. You're the coward behind the shooting of my cousin Lamar. You're the punk that went and tortured a woman trying to find me. Well, mutha'fucka, here I am," Hannibal stated as he took a step closer to Cee-Lo.

"You don't know who you're fuckin' wit'. Killin' me is only gonna make shit worse for you," Cee-Lo stated defiantly.

"I'll take my chances. What you need to be worried about is gettin' to a hospital so somebody can start tryin' to put your raggedy ass back together. I'll have someone call you an ambulance if you tell me who you work for," Hannibal said as he crossed his arms across his chest.

"I'm not tellin' you shit! I'm ready to die, so you might as well handle your business, nigga! You a coward anyway! You had to send a woman to do your dirty work! Is this the nigga you mutha'fucka's are willin' to follow to the grave?" Cee-Lo asked as he began to laugh and blood continued to pour from his disfigured face.

Danger stepped forward and without hesitation she sliced off Cee-Lo's left ear. He screamed out in pain as blood poured like it was coming from a water faucet from the side of his head. The alcohol that Cee-Lo had drank earlier that evening was causing his blood not to clot.

"If you start talkin' this can all be over with. We won't keep this goin'. We'll end this right now. I want to know who you work for. I don't know you but you obviously know me, so tell me what this is all about,"

Hannibal said as he looked at Cee-Lo with disgust written across his face.

The amount of blood that Cee-Lo was losing was beginning to take its toll on his body, and he was about to pass out before Danger reached in her pursue, pulled out a bottle of smelling sauce, and then ran it under where Cee-Lo's nose use to be located. Cee-Lo shook his head back and forth, trying to get away from the smell.

"Look, it's your boss we want not you. I'll let you go. You're no good to anyone anymore. You don't have a nose. You're blind. You can end all the pain if you just tell me who you work for," Hannibal said, trying his best to convince Cee-Lo to talk.

Cee-Lo shook his head no, but he didn't say anything. Danger walked over to the other side of the bed and she sliced Cee-Lo's other car off. This time Cee-Lo didn't scream due to the pain. He just let out a low groan and shook his head from side-to-side.

"Look, Hannibal, I know you enjoyin' this shit, but it's obvious this nigga ain't gonna talk. Just kill this mutha'fucka and let's get the fuck out of here. Ain't no tellin' who might of heard that nigga screamin'. We can get at these nigga's a different way," Bey jumped in and stated as he began to pace the floor.

"Fuck that! We need to find out what this nigga knows right now! If you scared or don't want to be here you can get the fuck out, nigga," Hannibal yelled with as he stared at Bey with rage in his eyes. "Now if you're worried about the nigga bein' heard why don't y'all tie what's left of this nigga's arms to the headboard and stuff one of those towels in this nigga's mouth. I'm not leavin' here until I get a name."

Lord Jamar and Gunslanger both stepped forward and did as Hannibal had instructed without hesitation.

"Now, since you can't talk, I want you to nod your fuckin' head if you're ready. Every time I ask you a question and you don't talk, I'm gonna have Danger cut somethin' else off. You ain't got a lot of shit left, so I would suggest you give it up quick. Now, who the fuck sent you down here to fuck with me?" Hannibal asked.

Cee-Lo grunted but he didn't nod his head. Danger quickly approached Cee-Lo and sliced his left big toe off. She did so with such force and precision that it flew and hit the wall across the room. Blood oozed from the hole in his foot like a slow running faucet.

"I'm gonna get a name out of you. What's the nigga's name and where do I find him?" Hannibal asked as he splashed a bottle of water in Cee-Lo's face to make sure he was still conscious and able to hear him.

Cee-Lo held his head up in the direction of the voice that he heard. Hannibal motioned for Danger to take the towel out of Cee-Lo's mouth so that he could talk.

Once the towel was removed, Cee-Lo defiantly stated, "Fuck you, mutha'fucka! I will see you in hell before I give up my people!"

"You will get there way before me, nigga. Tell me who sent you up here to try to fuck with us 'cause I have to admit you are good at what you do. Shit, if you weren't so fucked up I might hire you."

Cee-Lo still stood his ground and said nothing so Danger quickly cut off three of his fingers. Cee-Lo huffed and puffed but neither his head or tongue moved.

"Ok, I'm really enjoying seeing you being taken apart piece by piece, but I'm running out of time and patience. If you don't give me an answer the next time I ask you, I'm gonna have Danger cut off somethin' else. Only the next thing she cuts off is gonna be that little mutha'fucka hangin' between your legs, and even if you should be able to get some help before you bleed out, I can't think of one man that wants to travel this earth without a dick."

Hannibal waited to let his words sink in. Danger approached Cee-Lo and snatched his dick into her hand, and then held the blade against it so that he could feel what was about to happen if he didn't speak up.

Cee-Lo jerked his head up, and said, "Alright! Alright, I'll talk! How do I know you won't kill me anyway?"

"You don't, mutha'fucka!" Hannibal stated quickly. "But what you can guarantee is that if you don't talk I will kill you."

"His name is Ace," Cee-Lo stated as he gasped for air. "Twin was one of his best friends. He wants you all dead and that is why I'm here. You fucked with the wrong nigga. He won't stop, and you can't get to him so game over mutha'fucka," Cee-Lo stated with a slight chuckle.

Danger jerked her blade into the air to deliver the final blow, but Hannibal waved her off.

"Where do I find this, Ace?" Hannibal asked as he continued to stare at Cee-Lo with nothing but hate in his weary eyes.

"He works out of Miami, but you can't touch him. You and anybody associated with you is a dead man walkin'," Cee-Lo said as he shook his head back in forth to keep from passing out.

"Thanks for the information, homie. Now, like I said I'm gonna let you go," Hannibal walked over and shoved the washcloth back into Cee-Lo's mouth. "Danger, send this nigga to hell first class. Cut off his dick and balls, and then shove them down his throat. Slit his throat from ear-to-ear too. I want the message to be loud and clear when his so-called friends hear about this."

Hannibal turned and walked out of the suite without a second thought as Danger got to work dissecting Cee-Lo's body. When Danger was done, she was covered in blood. She helped herself to a hot shower, got dressed, and exited the suite with the stealth of a snake.

ELEVEN

Downstairs in the lobby of the hotel, Detectives Hightower and Livingston mulled over how they were going to be able to locate Hannibal and his crew without going through the proper police channels.

"So, Hightower, being that this was your bright idea, how do you suggest we go about finding these mutha'fucka's in this big son of a bitch?" Detective Livingston asked as he looked at his partner with a questioning smirk written across his face.

"I want to see the security tape. We can follow them right up to the room. That makes the most sense to me," Detective Hightower said as he started over to the front desk.

Detective Livingston grabbed Detective Hightower by the arm, and asked, "Do you remember that we don't have a warrant for this shit?"

"Since when has the Tulsa Police Department not done shit 'cause of a fuckin' warrant? All this shit is illegal until we call it in so fuck it. We need some probable cause for a warrant, so let's go get some probable cause. Now, let my fuckin' arm go and just follow my lead, detective," Detective Hightower stated as he jerked his arm away from his partner and continued to make his way towards the front desk.

Detective Livingston turned and followed behind his partner as he shook his head in disbelief. When they approached the front desk, Detective Hightower cleared his throat to get the attention of the front desk clerk who had her back turned to them.

"Sorry, welcome to the Doubletree Hotel. How may I help you gentlemen tonight?" the front desk clerk asked with a smile.

Detective Hightower flashed his detective's badge, and then said, "We are conducting an active investigation into a murder that occurred a couple months ago, and we have reason to believe that the perps are somewhere in your hotel. We need to check the names on your guest log, and we also need to take a look at your surveillance video in order to confirm that."

"Sir, I'm not authorized to give you access to that any of that, but I will get the hotel manager for you. Please wait just one second," the front desk clerk stated as she picked up the phone next to her and dialed an extension. "Ma'am, I have two police detectives out here that really need to speak with you," she said, and then paused to listen to her manager's reply. "Ok, I will let them know," she stated before she hung up the phone. "The manager said that she will be right out to speak with you all. If you would please have a seat, I'll send her right over to you when she comes out."

"If it is ok with you, we'll just stand right over there," Detective Hightower stated as he pointed to his right and began to move in that direction.

The detectives were so distracted that they failed to notice Hannibal and his crew as they made their way out of the front sliding doors towards their cars. The detectives waited two minutes before Detective Hightower's patience ran out.

"Excuse me, miss, but I need you to pick up that fuckin' phone and tell your manager to get her tight ass out here right now. Were in pursuit of a murderer for Christ sake," Detective Hightower stated before he slammed his hand down on the counter angrily.

"Sir, I'm going to have to ask that you refrain from using that type of language in our lobby. She will be right with you gentlemen," the front desk clerk stated as she gave them both a fake smile.

Just as she finished her comment the back office door swung open and the manager came walking through it. She looked to her left and then to her right before she noticed the two detective's waiting for her. She came from around the counter and approached them both with her hand extended to greet them.

Detective Livingston took her hand in his and as he did so the manager said, "I'm sorry to have kept the two of you waiting. How can we be of assistance to the Tulsa Police Department this evening?"

Detective Livingston released her hand and she extended it to Detective Hightower. He was so upset with the fact that he'd had to wait that he simply looked down at her hand then looked her back in the face.

"As we told the clerk over there, we are investigating a murder that took place a couple month's ago. We have reason to believe that the perps are somewhere in your hotel at this time. We would like permission to go through your current guest list and we would also like to check some of your surveillance video to see if we can spot them on it," Detective Hightower stated.

"The privacy of our guest is of our utmost concern here at the Doubletree Hotel, and even though I would like to do everything I can to help you, unless you have a warrant I am afraid that I can't allow you access to our guest list or our surveillance video," the hotel manager stated as she shook her head back and forth.

"Look lady, I can go get a warrant if you need me to but that could take hours at this time of night. In the meantime, a murderer might be running loose in your hotel. Do you want to be responsible when this psycho kills somebody here?" Detective Hightower paused before he continued. "I didn't think so. Now, you can be part of the problem or part of the solution. Let me see what I need to before this shit gets out of hand," Detective Hightower said in the most convincing way he could.

Detective Livingston just stared at the manager and hoped that she was willing to play ball. He had ten years on the force, and a wife who was pregnant. He didn't want to lose his job, his pension, or his freedom pursuing an illegal investigation with his overzealous partner.

"I'm going to allow this, but you need to make this quick. If you should find the guy your looking for on any of this, I will have to demand that you get the proper documentation before going after him. Is that clear?" the hotel manager asked as she looked back and forth at the two detectives.

"We can agree to that," Detective Hightower stated.

"Let me get our head of security down here so he can walk one of you through the surveillance footage while one of you takes a look at the guest log," the hotel manager suggested as she turned to walk back around the desk to use the phone.

"Detective Livingston, I'm going to check the video while you go with her and look at the guest log. Let me know if you see any name you might recognize, and I'll let you know if I see these assholes on the video. Remember, stay off the radio until we know somethin'," Detective Hightower instructed.

The hotel manager got the head of security to take Detective Hightower back to the video surveillance room and she also printed out a current guest list for Detective Livingston to review. After about an hour, Detective Hightower was able to spot Hannibal and his crew as they left the hotel. He backed tracked with the video and saw the room number that they left from before they made their exit. By that time it was around midnight, Detective

Hightower grabbed his cell phone off his hip and placed a call to the chief of detectives to bring him update to date on their findings.

Chief Yarbrough picked up on the third ring, and said, "Hightower, this better be good 'cause I'm coming off of a fifteen hour day."

"Chief, me and Livingston have video of our suspect in the Alex Whibley a.k.a Twin murder leaving the Doubletree Hotel earlier tonight. We also have reason to believe that him and his crew had something to do with those murders that took place earlier this evening. We also think that they were up to illegal active here at the hotel. We need your permission and a warrant to search the room that they were in before they left," Detective Hightower stated before putting his hand over the phone so that he could speak to the security guard that was standing nearby without the chief hearing him. "Do me a favor. Go get my partner and bring him here," Detective Hightower requested before he returned his attention back to the chief.

"Hightower, you and Livingston aren't on duty tonight and those murders happened a couple hours ago, so what are you and Livingston doing investigating a murder on your night off, and then trying to make a connection to another set of murders that you should have only heard about on the news? And if you had a solid lead why am I just now being informed? This better not be another one of your fucked up goose chases, Hightower 'cause if it is I'm gonna have your ass busted back to traffic duty," Chief Yarbrough warned as he walked over to the chair that sat in the corner of his room, grabbed his robe off of the arm, and then put it on.

"Chief, this is solid or I wouldn't be botherin' you. Just give us the warrant and let us do our job," Detective Hightower replied just as Livingston was walking through the door.

"Alright, let me make a call to the duty judge. You'll have your warrant in an hour or so, and I'm calling for a couple of uniforms to assist you," Chief Yarbrough stated before he ended the call.

"I understand chief. I will report back as soon as we know something," Detective Hightower before he pressed the end button on his cell phone. Detective Hightower turned to Detective Livingston, and said, "That was the chief on the phone. I was able to spot the scumbags leaving the hotel and trace them back to a room on the seventh floor. The warrant is on the way right now along with some back up. We're about to blow this case wide open."

"That sounds good to me 'cause I didn't find shit on the guest log," Detective Livingston stated as he ran his hand across his face.

"Well, fuck the guest log. The case is in room seven-thirteen," Detective Hightower proclaimed. "While we wait I'm gonna need a copy of this tape and I want to know who paid for that room. I also want a copy of the video when they checked in," Detective Hightower told the head of security.

The head of security did as Detective Hightower requested, and just about an hour later a couple uniformed officer arrived with the warrant. The detectives showed the warrant to the hotel manager and she willingly gave them a key to room seven-thirteen. Upon entering the room, they were horrified at what they found. Cee-Lo lifeless body laid sprawled across the bed. Blood was still was still oozing from his wounds so they knew he had not been dead long. His mouth hung open with his dick and balls hanging from his lips. Danger did as instructed and sliced his throat from ear-to-ear. She pulled his tongue through the wound, leaving it hanging down like a necktie. This was a tactic used on snitches by the Russian mob. Hannibal had read about in a book and that it would be a fitting message for

Cee-Lo's friends. He wanted them to know that he had broken Cee-Lo and that he planned to break them too.

Detective Hightower ordered that the room be sealed off until the medical examiner and the crime unit arrived. He didn't want any evidence to be disturbed. Now that he could tie Hannibal and his crew to the room, he had enough evidence to get murder warrants on all of them. Detective Hightower recognized each of the men, but he could not place the beautiful young lady that was with them. He would have to run her face through the system to try to identify her.

Detective Hightower phoned the chief and told him what they had found. He ordered them to both have their reports on his desk first thing in the morning. He also told them to immediately issue murder warrants for all of the five individuals that were seen exiting that room. He wanted their apprehension to be made a priority for the department. The media hadn't gotten wind of this murder yet, and the chief wanted to try and keep it that way. If they did get wind of it he wanted it to be because they had Hannibal and company in handcuffs and charged with murder.

"We got his ass now, and we get to bring the rest of those mutha'fucka's along for the ride, partner," Detective Hightower stated proudly.

"That sounds great. I'll put all their names out on a citywide, and I'll run the broads picture through facial recognition and see if we get a hit," Detective Livingston stated as he prepared to leave and head back to the station. "It looks like we're pullin' an all-nighter."

"Your damn right. Neither one of us is gonna rest until we bring these mutha'fucka's in. Let's get the hell out of here, and let these guy finish cleaning up. We've got a lot of work to do," Detective Hightower stated as they started for the door.

TWELVE

Knock! Knock!

Hannibal jumped with alertness at the sound of someone banging on the front door Lamar's condo. He instinctively grabbed his .40 caliber Desert Eagle and tiptoed to the door so he could see through the peephole.

"Man, what the fuck is Andrea doing over here?" Hannibal whispered under his breath to himself.

Andrea was standing far enough away from the door for Hannibal to be able to see that she was wearing a black full length trench coat and high heel pumps.

Knock! Knock! Knock! Knock!

Andrea impatiently banged again on Lamar's door, noticing a shadow being cased over the peephole which told her someone was inside and just not opening the door.

"Well, what's up stranger?" Hannibal greeted her with a curious grin after opening the door, and then peeking around her to check for any foul play.

"Well, hello to you Mr. Can't-Be-Found," Andrea responded playfully with a warm smile, fighting the urge to lose focusing concerning killin' Hannibal who was the very man she was falling in love with.

"I guess I deserved that," Hannibal commented with a giggle as he cracked a guilty smile, allowing himself to relax a bit. "Anyway, how did you know that I was over here?"

"Before we even get into all of that, are you gonna invite me in the house or do you want to stand here at the door all day?" Andrea asked, giving Hannibal a look of displeasure, and then she placed her hands on her hips and stared into his eyes.

"Damn, my bad, boo! Come on in," Hannibal stated as he stepped to the side, allowing Andrea to walk pass him into the condo as he watched her phat ass jingle.

Hannibal closed the door behind Andrea. When he turned around to face her she removed the trench coat, exposing that up under it she was only wearing a black laced thong with a matching black laced bra.

"Damn, girl, you crazy as hell," Hannibal stated with a laugh.

"Now, to answer your question, Sharel told me that you was over here, which is why I came prepared to make up for lost time. Do you have a problem with that?" Andrea asked seductively as she looked at Hannibal with lust in her eyes.

Andrea put her hands on her hips, exposing her curvaceous body to Hannibal with hopes that he would fall into her trap.

"Nah, it's cool. You look fine as wine right now," Hannibal charmingly replied with a slight grin, feeling an instant hard on at the sight of Andrea licking her lips while rubbing her fingers in between her legs with one hand and motioning for him to come to her with the other hand.

"Did you miss me?" Andrea whispered into Hannibal's ear in the sexiest tone of voice she could muster.

Andrea started to kiss Hannibal on his lips, ears, and neck while she slow removed his shirt and jeans.

"You know I missed you," Hannibal lied as he breathed in deeply.

The truth was that Hannibal had been so busy with trying to find out who was after him and his crew that he had not had the time to give Andrea a second thought. Anticipating Andrea's next move, Hannibal removed his boxers himself, and then she grabbed his dick in her hands and began to stroke it seductively.

Then out of nowhere, Andrea snatched Hannibal to the floor, positioning him on his back and began to suck his dick slowly as she squeezed his balls aggressively.

"Oh, baby, that shit feels good!" Hannibal proclaimed with joy.

His words sent a rush of pleasure through Andrea, ending between her legs as her pussy became dripping wet.

"Close your eyes, baby," Andrea instructed deceivingly as she continued to tease the head of his dick with her tongue.

"Damn, you on some freaky shit tonight," Hannibal stated as he complied with Andrea's request, and then he leaned his head back.

Hannibal began to feel a rush of cum rising to the head of his dick, forcing him to grab the back of Andrea's head and start to move her mouth faster-and-faster on his dick.

Hannibal moaned loudly, and shouted, "Oh, baby, I'm cummin'!"

"Cum in momma's mouth, baby!" Andrea shouted back as she removed Hannibal's hands from her head and placed them by his side, while continuing to suck on his dick as she removed her thong.

Suddenly Andrea stopped, leaving Hannibal anxious for more. She then positioned herself on top of his dick and began to ride him like a pro as she removed the small blade that was taped to her side, and eased it up to Hannibal's throat.

"What do you think you're doing, bitch?" Hannibal yelled out just before she swiped the blade across his throat in a classic attempt to take his life.

Just then, Hannibal woke up from a deep but traumatic sleep in a cold sweat. He was short of breath and shaking. His mind replayed the visions in his dream and he began to wonder if this dream was a sign of events to come or if he was becoming paranoid due to all of the things that were taking place around him.

The next few weeks would be more important than any that he had ever experienced in his life. He would be going after a man that had managed to take out or seriously wound three people who were very important to him, not to mention the attempts that had been made on his life. Now, he felt that he was receiving premonitions that Andrea, a woman that he felt he could love for the rest of his life, was the poison that could be his downfall.

Hannibal sat on the couch in his cousin's condo and again he wondered if this life was worth it. He questioned would life have been different for him had he not chased the material things that he now had. He questioned are the life's and happiness of his friends and family worth the richest that he coveted.

Hannibal quickly pushed those thought to the back of his mind when he heard his cell phone ringing. He saw it was Dee. He was glad to see that it was him because his business with Dee and Wind was the last thing he had to do before he also left town.

He answered on the third ring, and said, "Dee, I'm glad you called. I know you heard about Lamar so shit got a little hectic around here. When can we meet up and get shit squared away?"

"We need to do this sooner rather than later 'cause our friend is ready to hit the highway. Plus, we both want our money," Dee stated.

"Have you ever had to worry 'bout gettin' your money from me?" Hannibal asked with a little irritation in his voice.

"No, but—" Dee started to say before Hannibal cut him off.

"Well, don't start worrying now. I got both y'all's money and its more to come if you want it. So, just calm your nerves and tell me where you want to meet 'cause I need to make this to happen sooner than later too."

"Meet us at the same place we met the first time. Lacy Park by the swimming pool. Come by yourself and make sure you're not followed. Be there at eight o'clock in the morning," Dee stated before he ended the call.

At seven-fifty a.m. Hannibal sat in the parking lot waiting for Dee and Wind. He knew that he needed to hurry because he wanted to be on the road before the shit hit the fan about the bodies in the house and at the Doubletree Hotel. He wanted to be in another city where his name didn't ring out the streets so he would be more difficult to find. Dee and Wind arrived at exactly eight o'clock, and they pulled into the parking spot next to Hannibal.

Hannibal got out of his Mercedes-Benz and he was carrying a small black bag in his left hand. He slow walked to the front of his car and so did Dee and Wind.

"Let's skip the pleasantries 'cause we all know each other here. Wind, I want to say that I appreciate the way you took care of that piece of business for me. I have y'all's money right here in this bag. There is fifty grand in there for Wind and another twenty-five grand in there for you," Hannibal stated as he pointed towards Dee.

"Do we need to count it?" Wind asked with a slight grin.

"You can do that when you're wastin' your own time counting it not mine. I have more money where that came from if y'all want to put in the work to get it," Hannibal stated, and then he pushed the bag over the hood of the car towards Dee.

"What do you have in mind?" Wind asked.

Dee already had an idea about what Hannibal wanted them to do so he just stood and said nothing.

"My cousin and some people close to me were shot after we killed some punk ass niggas a few months ago. I've come to find out those niggas were connected to some big wig in Miami named Ace, and now he is coming after me and anyone close to me. I want that mutha'fucka dead, and I want y'all to do it. I will give y'all as much help as I can but the job is yours to do. I don't care how you get it done. The price tag is two hundred thousand. Do we have a deal?" Hannibal asked as looked back and forth at them for conformation.

Dee spoke up, and said, "Man, you know I'm down, but you know this shit is gonna take a little bit of time. It ain't like we fuckin' wit' a nigga from around here, but you know any nigga can get got."

"I'll take the job but I work alone. I don't need no help. If you want the nigga dead, he's dead," Wind stated without a blink of an eye.

"Ok, I can deal with that, but if you need help you know where to find it. Dee, I want you to stay here and ensure Lamar's safety while he recovers. I'm puttin' his life in your hands from this moment on. Wind will call you if he needs you, and you call me if he needs me. My new phone number is in the bag. Memorize the number, and then burn it. No matter what, I want this shit done in three months or less so you on the clock starting right now," Hannibal said before he turned to walk back towards his car door. Hannibal opened the driver's side door, and then said, "I'm paying y'all twice what the goin' rate is for this one 'cause failure is not an option. I want y'all to earn ever fuckin' penny," Hannibal stated before he got inside of his Mercedes-Benz and sped out of the parking lot without looking back.

Hannibal went back to Lamar's condo, and by noon he was ready to hit the highway. He didn't know where he was going, but he knew it needed to be somewhere that would allow him to relax and think. He had a lot on his mind and he needed sometime away from it all. He had several different things to worry about all at the same time.

He had to worry about Lamar's health and the chance that the people that shot him might come back to finish the job. He had to worry about another member of Hustla'z Inc. being killed or hurt during a war that he had no intention on starting. He had to worry about being away from his base of operations for an extended period of time and someone trying to move in on what is his. He also had to worry about going to jail behind all the bodies that he was leaving behind in the midst of this war with a nigga he only knew by the name of Ace.

Beyond it all, Hannibal knew he was already in it too deep to turn back, and the only way he knew how to play the game was to win. The only difference this time was that not only was his freedom on the line but his very existence was also in jeopardy.

TO BE CONTINUED...

A HUSTLA'Z LIFE

Hannibal, a young man from Tulsa, Oklahoma, grows up wanting some of the finer things in life. Due to the fact that his family cannot afford those things, he decides to take matters into his own hands.

Hannibal begins a life of crime that turns into a life of turmoil. He is the leader of the biggest crime mob in Oklahoma, however he wants to do other things besides just rob, steal, and kill.

When he is convicted of a jewelry store robbery, Hannibal is give an ultimatum by the judge. He is told that he is not to commit any type of illegal act for one hundred and twenty days or he will be sentenced to numerous years in state prison with no questions asked.

Will he go to prison or will he be able to stay out of trouble and retain his freedom while continuing to reign supreme over his criminal empire?

Only A Hustla'z Life will tell.

COMING SOON IN KINDLE AND PAPERBACK VERSIONS

Thank you
for your support. Don't
forget to leave a
review!

CPSIA information can be obtained
at www.ICGtesting.com
Printed in the USA
LVHW050022160122
708681LV00019B/1645

9 781976 325366